THE WHITE SHIP
Estonian Tales

THE WHITE SHIP
Estonian Tales by
AINO KALLAS

Translated from the Finnish by
ALEX MATSON
With a Foreword by
JOHN GALSWORTHY

Short Story Index Reprint Series

BOOKS FOR LIBRARIES PRESS
FREEPORT, NEW YORK

First Published 1924
Reprinted 1971

INTERNATIONAL STANDARD BOOK NUMBER:
0-8369-3948-4

LIBRARY OF CONGRESS CATALOG CARD NUMBER:
73-163034

PRINTED IN THE UNITED STATES OF AMERICA

Foreword

ONE APOLOGIZES FOR WRITING words of introduction to stories so strong, so full of atmosphere, so individual in method as these. To write a foreword is an invidious task anyway, and personally I don't believe such introductions serve any purpose. Authors don't like the feeling that they are required ; critics resent incentives to approval ; the Public doesn't read them. They are *inania verba*—but for some occult reason publishers still attach importance to them.

Madame Aino Kallas, though well-known elsewhere, is so far, unfortunately, unknown by us in England. Judged by at least half these stories she is one of the strongest and most individual of living writers. Reading them, one is conscious of a new dish—of a strange flavour, and of coming very close to primal things. " The Death of Org," " Gerdruta Carponai," " The Legend of Young Odele and the Leper," " Ingel," " The Rye Field," are not easily matched. " The Sacrifice " is a perfect little masterpiece.

Madame Aino Kallas is Finnish. She writes of Estonia, her husband's country, of a tragic

people in a strange, sea-girt setting.   Her method
is singularly simple, clean, and direct ; her sense
of atmosphere remarkable.

Though I maintain that they are unnecessary,
I am proud to write these few words about work
for which I feel such genuine admiration.

JOHN GALSWORTHY

Preface

THE CENTRAL BLACK STRIPE IN the blue-black-and-white flag of the Estonian Republic has certainly not come there by chance. It symbolizes effectively the clear streak of suffering which runs through all the chronicles of this people. Few indeed are the nations of Europe whose struggle for liberty has been as hard-fought as that of Estonia.

The position of Estonia as a thorough-fare betwixt East and West, made it a field for devastating wars through all history.

So placed, on an area larger than that of Denmark or Holland, bounded to the north and west by the Baltic Sea and its gulfs, eastward by Russia, and southward by what is now the Republic of Latvia, the Estonians have dwelt for fifteen centuries. It speaks much for the toughness of this race that, despite its history, only seven per cent. of its present population are of alien race. Ethnographically, the Estonians are related to the Finns and the Hungarians, with whom they form together the Finno-Ugric language-group.

The old Estonians were an extremely liberty-loving and warlike people, daring and enterprising, living chiefly by agriculture and maritime commerce, but addicted also to piracy, their raids ſtretching to the coaſts of Sweden. The level of their civilization was approximately that of the other Baltic countries. Before the German conqueſt they had advanced almoſt to the modern conception of a State, being governed by " Elders " chosen from amongſt the people and possessing an organized military force. Their fortifications of earth and ſtone have survived in many cases to the present day.

The introduction of Chriſtianity in the beginning of the thirteenth century—by fire and sword—marks an epoch in Eſtonian hiſtory. After a bloody and furious resiſtance of over a century the country fell at laſt to the German Knights of the Sword, an Order of Knighthood founded with the Papal blessing expressly for the subjugation and conversion of the Baltic lands.

The results of this conqueſt were disaſtrous to the Eſtonians. The land tilled for centuries by their anceſtors was divided among German bishops and Knights of the Order, the people themselves deprived of the commoneſt rights and ruled with a harshness that, according to neutrals, was without parallel in the whole of Europe.

The Estonian peasant became the property, body and soul, of his German lord. Without possessions, tied, *glebae adscriptus*, to the soil on which he laboured, his status was no whit better than that of an animal or an inanimate object. Children had no right of inheritance ; on the death of a peasant his scanty chattels became the property of the lord of the manor. The highest judicial powers were held by estate-owners within their respective areas. That peasants were whipped to death was no uncommon occurrence, nor was the *jus primæ noctis* unknown. Peasants were sold or bartered for other property —cases where peasants were exchanged for a hound are known—husbands were parted from wives, families torn asunder. Punishment by the whip was usual for the most trifling fault.

Meanwhile the country passed from the hands of one conqueror to another. The year 1562 saw the overthrow of the German Order and a partition of Estonia between Sweden, Poland and Denmark. Peter the Great conquered the country in 1710, laying waste its towns and villages until his military commander could truthfully report : " there is nothing more to destroy." For two hundred years Estonia became a part of the Great Russian Empire.

Through all these major struggles the Estonian peasant remained in the bondage his original conquerors had imposed on him. Sanguinary attempts at revolt, which occurred with fateful regularity each century, proved powerless to effect any improvement in his status. Not until the new eighteenth-century ideals of liberty and fraternity had gained a temporary victory in Europe were voices heard demanding the abolition of slavery in the Baltic Provinces. Current opinion, backed by the Russian Government, finally forced the Baltic aristocracy, in 1816 and 1819, to grant some measure of liberty to the unfortunate Estonians.

Actually, the new liberty existed more or less on paper. The concessions of 1816 and 1819 served only to plunge the peasant into deeper misery. He was free in that the responsibility of feeding him no longer rested on his master, but being deprived of the wherewithal of agrarian existence, land, he was still at the mercy of the large estate-owner, to whom the hitherto unappropriated residue of land was now transferred. Rents for the use of land were extracted not in money, but in labour and kind. Serfdom had been replaced by labour-slavery. Corporal punishment still flourished. The general dissatisfaction was so great that about the year 1840 great numbers of Estonians went over from the Lutheran to the Greek Orthodox Church—the Czar's Church—in the hope of bettering their condition, or migrated to Russia.

A dismal history, the history of the land in Estonia, on which I have purposely dwelt at such length as it forms the background for the majority of the stories in this collection.

The national and cultural awakening of Estonia in the modern sense of these terms dates from the middle of last century. The abolition of labour-slavery in 1862 brought in its train the right for a peasant to purchase land—the land wrested forcibly from his ancestors—or to pay land rents in money. This denoted the rise of a class of free Estonian peasantry, and a period of material and spiritual development now began which was to lift the nation out of its unmerited degradation. A growing stream of Estonians found the road to higher education open to them, and an educated class gradually formed, without the Germanization which previously had been a corollary to education : a powerful Estonian element penetrated into the towns. From small beginnings an Estonian press, an Estonian literature were created. Even the years of forcible Russification, from 1885 onward, when all teaching, in elementary schools and Universities alike, had to be done in Russian, and in Law Courts and all Government services the only language was Russian, could no longer hinder the forward march of the idea of Estonian liberty, the seven hundred year old dream of the race.

The period of crisis following the Great War found Estonia fully ripe for independence : on February 24, 1918, the country was declared an independent Republic. Many trials had still to be endured, however, before the young Republic could settle down to a peaceful reorganization of its conditions : a German occupation, a war lasting a year against Soviet Russia, a further struggle against the German Landeswehr under von der Goltz, struggles during which the appearance of British naval units outside Tallinn awakened an enthusiasm equalled only by the enthusiasm with which the Finnish volunteers were received.

The sufferings outlined above are now ancient history. The present Estonia is a flourishing Republic, acknowledged *de jure* by all the leading nations and a member of the League of Nations. Its finances are in order, its exchange ſtabilized, its export continually increasing. The land, source of so much misery has been divided amongſt the tillers of the soil, with twofold results : the dangers of an agrarian proletariat have been averted, and a faſt bulwark created againſt Bolshevism. Intellectually, the pulse of life is equally ſtrong, as witness the ſtream of ſtudents to the Eſtonian University of Tartu—" With the fainteſt tinge of dawn, the Eſtonian repaired without delay the walls of his ruined home and ploughed his weeded fields," writes an Eſtonian hiſtorian.

At the moment the Eſtonian is rebuilding the whole of his home, from its foundations upwards. Here is a people that desires to live, and has shown its vitality.

A word of explanation yet as to the ſtories in this volume. The majority are the outcome of the spirit of opposition awakened in one coming from the comparative freedom of Finland by the feudal atmosphere that until recently prevailed in Eſtonia. Few only of the ſtories are entirely imaginative. Sad to say almoſt all are based on aċtual incidents. The ſtories " The Wedding," "Ingel," " A Bathsheba of Saaremaa," " The Trip to Town," " The Parish Clerk and the Vicar," " The Death of Kubja Pärt,"

"The White Ship," and "The Sacrifice," are, like the description of Saaremaa, from the period of labour-slavery in Estonia, about the middle of last century. "Bernhard Riives" and "The Death of Org" describe the terrors of the Revolution of 1905, when the attempts of the Estonian peasants to shake off the shackles of feudalism resulted in the importation by the Baltic estate-owners of a Cossack punitive force.

SAAREMAA, EESTI 11. VIII. 23.   AINO KALLAS

Contents

	PAGE
SAAREMAA	17
THE LEGEND OF YOUNG ODELE AND THE LEPER	22
GERDRUTA CARPONAI	36
A BATHSHEBA OF SAAREMAA	54
THE WEDDING	69
INGEL	80
THE DEATH-BED OF KUBJA-PÄRT	94
THE TRIP TO TOWN	100
THE PARISH CLERK AND THE VICAR	114
THE SACRIFICE	128
THE SMUGGLER	139
ALIEN BLOOD	154
THE RYE-FIELD	168
A LOVE STORY	177
THE STRANGER	189
BERNHARD RIIVES	198
THE DEATH OF ORG	207
THE WHITE SHIP	225

Saaremaa

SAAREMAA, ISLAND OF SLAVES . . .
Open pasturages, sandy moors where the
villagers' cattle graze in the summers. Miles of
level, treeless plain, lying open to the sun which
slowly scorches it, withering the grass to a short,
tangled outcrop on the face of the earth. The
clayey, grey soil is cracked with drought, wrinkled
with deep crevices and folds like the skin of the
aged. Not a tree offers shade ; the earth is as
hard as rock, even a cloudburst hardly penetrates
it, and the water remains on its surface in little
brown streams. After rain the ground is alive
with snails, creeping slowly forward, bearing
their houses on their backs.

Already before midsummer, all vegetation has
gone ; only the juniper with tough insistence
still drives its roots into the sun-baked earth.
But the hungry droves of sheep, who leave behind
them not a single seed-leaf, attack even the
juniper's prickly branches. Gnawing from all
sides at the bushes they reduce them to large
green hummocks, set side by side on the level
ground. They stand as it were in a rococo
garden, clipped into decorative form by the
hand of a skilful gardener, some round as spheres,

others elongated like eggs, others shaped to resemble onions, or the cupolas of Russian churches. Between these juniper-bushes only thorns can grow and a tiny red flower whose fiery, creeping clusters glow in the withered green like showers of sparks.

The landscape improves progressively—the cattle plains give way to moors covered with hazel-bushes, where swollen with pride the juniper achieves the status of a tree, and looks like a poor stunted copy of the cypresses in the graveyard groves of the south. A low ridge of hills crosses the road, a target for the ceaseless onslaught of the winds, which, as though bent on wiping it out, constantly sweep from its crest great clouds of white flying sand, so that, over the whole neighbourhood, the passer-by seems to be sinking into a bed of sawdust.

Soon the farms and the huts of Saaremaa begin to appear on both sides of the road, at times singly, hiding among the bushes or scattered over the stone-strewn flats, or gathered into hamlets, five or six houses in a cluster. Always they are humble and low-ceiled—steep roofs of turf or straw shading the walls like a hat drawn deep down over a man's eyes. They crouch as close to the ground as possible, as though to attract a minimum of attention, hardly distinguishable in their everlasting grey colouring from the surrounding soil. Even when they combine into villages they are still timid and fearful, as though fear had driven a half-dozen of huts to seek protection together. Blackened and dilapidated, a dwelling-house, threshing-barn and cattle-shed under one roof, they cower beneath their impossible roofs, which seem about to choke and crush all life out of the hut beneath. Here and there a windmill, on a round base of stone, slowly cuts the air with its grey wings.

The heart of Saaremaa is of stone. When the land cracks during the spring floods and rains, it lays bare whitey-green limestone, the bone beneath the deep open wounds of the earth. Of such is the backbone of Saaremaa.

Much history exists of Saaremaa, but Saaremaa itself is its own most impartial historian. The record of seven centuries of slavery is written upon its landscape.

The whole is crushed and meek, as though trampled for ages under an iron heel. For those with eyes to see—the starved, accusing features of a labour-slave stare from all quarters of the sun-baked, unworked pasturage.

Even the Saaremaa rock mirrors a slavish soul,

never rising to the height of a mountain, never defying the heavens, but withdrawing into the earth, hiding its menace in its heart, like a slave. And the thorns of the grazing-moors, hardly visible on the ground, treacherously stab at your hand or foot, and for you they are too lowly to be punished even by breaking-off, but instead you walk on, thinking : " a thorn's revenge, the revenge of a slave ! "

Even the flower-time of Saaremaa is short and garish as a slave's holiday. A bare two weeks before midsummer its clover-fields wave in a sea of bright colour, rising luxuriant and tall. Then it is like a hothouse of the Baltic, filled by the winds that sweep it with rare flowers, scarcely known in the bleak north. The scythe is already prepared for it, a nerve-rending sound of sharpening is heard from every house, blades gleam at the corners of the huts—to-morrow or on its morrow the gay play of colour is extinguished. But the days ushering in midsummer are the bridal days of Saaremaa, a wealth of honeyed perfumes on the wind, a festal song sung in colour. Here is atonement for barren cattle-lands and hungry moors. Here are days when the land decks itself gaily, as the slaves that toil upon it deck themselves of a Sunday in their gay national dress, forgetting their weekday rags in a riot of bright-coloured attire. Beside the simple low fences of piled-up boulders the dog-rose flowers, transforming the dusty, dry roads into fresh gardens of roses, hiding their thorns cat-like beneath their red blooms. The water-logged lowlands wave their covering of white cotton-grass, soft as newly-fallen flakes of snow ; beside gushing springs forget-me-nots flourish, ever dwelling near to water, that they may wash their blue eyes clean. Here and there in the manor lanes, the white blossoms of the horse-chestnut peep out from the foliage, standing rigid and stiff on their branches like lighted clusters of candles. In the crevices between sandy ridges and stone fences, in the cracks of the thatched roofs even, yellow stone-crop clings fast, growing in thick patches like yellow lichen.

This is Saaremaa, the island of slaves . . .

The Legend of Young Odele and the Leper

ODELE, DAUGHTER OF VALDE-mar, the young alien-born wife of Jürgen Schutte, Councillor of the town of Tallinn, let fall into her lap the altar-cloth which at her husband's expressed wish she had been embroidering for the church of St. John's Hospital for Lepers.

She remembered all at once the new patient who was expected, and began to prepare the basket to welcome him, another request of her husband, who was head of the hospital. From a silver-mounted oaken trunk she took out linen bandages for the patient's sores and filled with them the bottom of the basket ; above them she laid two symbols of white wool shaped like hands, for the patient to bear as a sign of his disease. Above these she placed a slice of fresh pork, which was believed to possess healing powers. This was the councillor's gift to each new patient. A coffin had to be brought by the patient himself.

When all was ready, Odele called aloud for a serving-maid, but the house was empty, the servants having hurried to the market-place to see a strolling conjurer. Then Odele took her newly-awakened ten-month old son from his cradle, the first-born of her marriage, and departed with the child on her arm into the garden.

She settled herself in her favourite spot, a bench of stone, behind which rose-bushes in bloom grew against the wall. A shudder passed through her limbs. Always she felt cold, even in summer. For her there never could be too much sun. An arctic, cold and gloomy land, where the blood itself seemed to lose its colour from lack of sunshine.

It seemed to her at times that she was sick with longing for the country from which her parents had once, in a ship laden with merchandise, sailed to the mouth of the Düna. The country that she had seen only as a little child, lived in her thoughts enveloped in a shining mist, and she would beg traders from the Hansa towns to tell her of it. Doubtless more sun was there, and a merrier, more joyous people. There were green beech-woods, golden sand-flats and dazzlingly white cliffs of limestone, washed by the sea. The people spoke a softer lisping language, like the chatter of children, and were golden-haired, white and rose tinted. But deep in Odele's soul dwelt a secret doubt of those mirage-like visions, as though a single glance at the

23

reality would cause them to shrink to shapes of everyday and dissolve.

She sat, her long and finely-modelled throat bent back, her lips parted like a cloven berry, the paleness of a marsh-flower in her cheeks.

Odele accused herself bitterly at the moment. Her heart was hard and indifferent, empty of charity and merciful love. Loathing and disgust dwelt in it, in place of the pity and human love that befitted the daughter of a Christian Church and the wife of Jürgen Schutte. Was it not even now because she was compelled thereto that she set in order the basket and embroidered an altar-cloth for the lepers !

Ah, Odele hated the miserable wretches, whom her husband's occupation forced her so often to see. She heard of them incessantly, but could not bring herself to forgive her husband for having accepted the supreme control of the hospital. In the beginning she had constantly begged him to give up the post, but Jürgen Schutte's enthusiasm, on the other hand, had grown from day to day. Latterly, he had cared many times more for any matter connected with the Hospital of St. John than for all his duties as a Councillor of the town. He planned perpetually all kinds of improvements for the hospital ;

his ambition was to raise the institution that he controlled in all respects to the status of the model hospitals at Jerusalem, where patients were given fresh pork thrice each week. Recently, he had begun the building of a new hospital church, and further he intended building in the near future a smoke-stack for the Hospital of St. John, and even a stone bath-house, in place of the old one, destroyed four times by fire. He experimented with all kinds of new decoctions of herbs and new medicines. He was enterprising and energetic, always at work, so that he almost neglected his home, his wife and his infant child for the sake of these miserable outcasts.

Odele for her part could never banish her horror. It hurt her to see beyond the town the walls of the Hospital of St. John and before it the four pillars hollowed for alms, which were emptied at intervals by the monks. She became sick with dread whenever she heard from afar the faint clatter of the wooden rattles, carried by the lepers to warn the passers-by. She avoided her husband on his return from the hospital, crouching beneath the caress of his hand, which all too recently had been busied with the sores of lepers. She became in the end so afraid that she hardly dared touch the honey of bees, for

25

fear they might bring infection from the petals of flowers growing in the hospital garden. To Jürgen Schutte she never dared to confess the fact, but in secret she examined carefully her own body and that of the child, becoming panic-stricken at the slightest abrasion and bathing the child in fragrant balsams. Her dislike for the sick was unconquerable, and she never failed to show it whenever it proved impossible for her to avoid dealing with them, despite the prayers and stern rebukes of her husband and her own burning prayers, with which she perpetually besieged the Virgin Mary, begging that the indifference of her heart be lifted from her.

The heart of the young, alien-born wife of Jürgen Schutte had become timid and dreary in a strange country and in close propinquity to the doomed. Leaving the town on occasional short journeys into the country she was afraid of this newly-conquered Maarjamaa, denuded of male inhabitants, the remains of recently demolished fortifications still standing in the woods and marshes ; where she was met at every step by breeding, sorrowful women mourning the fallen and bearing at their breasts a new generation, enslaved even before birth. She could not shake off the fear that the former gods of the country, hungrily awaiting the blood of sacrifices that came not, might spread in their ire the seeds of plague and pestilence to all quarters of the earth, to the ruin of its inhabitants.

Odele loved to sit with the child in her arms, as she was doing now, and dream, but the life occupying her thoughts was such as existed nowhere. Certainly not in this vanquished, chilly land, perhaps also not elsewhere. Closing her eyes, Odele saw only beautiful people, who walked as kings or gods, and she felt that she belonged to these, to a land as yet uncreated and to a human race yet unborn.

Around Odele the talk turned always on war, all the men she knew having taken part in the crusade against the heathen peasantry. They spoke incessantly of great catapults or new-fashioned engines of siege ; sitting beside their tankards they boasted with glowing faces of their bloody deeds. They had broken this fiery mad race, which had refused to accept amicably the Holy Baptism and to give up its lands and forests. They had slaughtered it like cattle ; sought out its hiding places in marshes and wilds ; they had filled caves in the hills with hundreds of its men, women and children huddled together, and had lit bonfires at the cave

27

mouth, suffocating the heathen dogs like mos-
quitoes.

Or they disputed through the evenings over
the relative superiority of the Knights of the
Sword and the Bishops. Both had their parti-
sans, the Knights of the Sword, and the Bishops,
and the disputes could laſt until morning.

These discussions were a horror to Odele, a
weariness and a disguſt ; war she loved not—
even she abhorred it. But when inſtead of
knights and soldiers, men of the Church sat at
the Councillor's table, and fragments of the
speech of prieſts and monks penetrated to her
woman's ear, she underſtood them not one whit
better. They too argued, growing hot and
angry as they disputed. Their arguments were
concerned with such queſtions as whether angels
slept and ate, which some doubted and others
believed, so that they would have wagered their
eternal welfare upon the truth of these fancies ;
or else their disputes were spun round the com-
position of the human soul, of which warmth,
moiſture, air were elements.

Never had Odele heard other matters discussed than war and again war, wars paſt and
those to come, bickerings and hate, or else matters
purely celeſtial. And all alike seemed filled

with envy and quarrelsomeness to the verge of eruption, Knights of the Sword againſt the Church, German againſt Dane and contrariwise.

On the other hand, no one ever dreamed of talking, for variety's sake, of the roses growing againſt the wall ; only to the bees were these of account ! The prieſts cultivated their herbs solely to diſtil ointments from them or to ſteep them in the omnipotent holy water. And with the setting of the sun people prophesied rain or fine weather for their fields, or favouring winds or ſtorms for their merchantmen in the Baltic, the lighting of a ruddier blaze than usual in the Weſt inspiring them to forebodings of new plagues and spoilings. But not one was ſtruck by the speƈtacle of the sunset sky to silent awe, to forgetfulness of weather and rain, to oblivion of all else but the radiant play of colour in the sky.

And yet the matters occupying Odele's mind were vain and of profit to no one. All that flowered and drooped for its own sake alone, children for whom time was ſtill endless and eternal and who therefore knew no haſte, being nearer the primal secret of life ; dragon-flies, the blue rings on whose bodies, shining as the blue of heaven, she counted for her pleasure ;

so too the colours born in standing water, many tinted and melting as in the rainbow ; the roses on the wall.

But of all this she felt that she must keep silent. Only to her ten-month infant would she speak of these vain but delightful things, in tender lonely moments like the present hour on the stone bench warmed by the sun. Even the child would fail to understand her after a few years. He would sit as a scholar, the Latin Grammar of Ælius Donatus in his hand, forgetting his mother's tales of evening skies and roses. And one day he would be ready to appear before her in full martial array, with battle-axe girt to his side, on the road to deeds of blood. The hearts of mothers were created to be pierced by double-edged swords, even from Her who gave mortal shape to the Son of God.

The child moved in Odele's lap. Odele broke off a great red rose from the bushes beneath the wall, cleared it of thorns and put it in the child's hand.

Then came a knocking, repeated two or three times. The servants were evidently still away.

Odele rose therefore and with the child in her arms went to open the gate leading to the garden. She was slightly languid from the long sitting in the sun, on her lips played her usual timid and gentle smile.

Odele opened the gate. Outside, before her, two men were standing, one old and barefooted, the other still young, in the apparel of a leper, but without the rattle and the woollen hands.

" Art thou Odele, daughter of Valdemar, the wife of the Councillor ? " inquired the barefooted man.

" I am," Odele answered, " and the basket is ready."

And still carrying the child she returned to the building, took the newly-prepared basket and carried it to the gate.

" My husband, the Councillor Jürgen Schutte, sends thee this for thy immediate needs " she said, without looking at the leper. She was about to close the gate again, in the throes of the old unconquerable antipathy in the presence of a leper, when suddenly a broken though still young voice uttered :

" Woman, thou whom men call Odele, be merciful and have pity, as the Mother of the Lord. The leper begs the rose in thy hand."

Despite her recent prayers, an unbearable pain took possession of Odele. Never would she

31

grow used to this sight. Never would she be able to serve these forsaken of God.

And in confusion, with downcast glance, she said :

" A rose ? Why dost thou beg a needless and trivial rose ? What wouldst thou with a flower ? "

The leper answered :

" Nothing. But neither is it necessary to thee. Hundreds such grow in thy garden."

Odele, in greater confusion, made reply :

" A rose ? But why a rose ? See, I have brought thee the basket. Later thou wilt receive more, my husband looking after thee as his child. Here are soft bandages for thy sores, of the finest linen. Here is fresh pork for thee to eat and become well."

And a sudden keen desire to praise her husband and his works for the Hospital of St. John arose in Odele. It was as though she herself was for the first time made aware of the activities and the generosity of her husband.

The leper said again in his voice broken by disease :

" I thank thee, woman, Odele is thy name ? Thou art then from a far country ? Thou hast prepared everything beyond praise. But give me the rose in the hand of thy child."

32

Odele began to breathe deeply, a great unrest pulsing in her veins.

"I do not understand thee," she said, "I do not understand why thou desirest the rose. I have heard men speak of war and catapults, but never of roses. If thou so wishest, I will send word to my husband that he may increase thy daily provision? He is a Councillor and the best of men. He has intended to give thee fresh pork thrice each week, as is done in Jerusalem. Is not that enough? If thou wishest, I will beg him not to build the dungeon for the mutinous and defiant among you. The Councillor is just, though hot in wrath. Dost thou wish me to beg for better garments, the bath more frequently for thee?"

The bees hummed in the garden, all else was silence, and then the leper replied:

"Woman, there was a time when I desired all that was pleasant on the earth. No joy was there but my senses had revelled in it. I have filled my brain with all the learning of our time, I have borne armour as a soldier; women have heaped on me their love, from princess to scullery maid. All that is past, the curse of God weighs heavily on me, and all I desire is the rose in the hand of thy child. Not even thee, Odele, do I desire, though with these dim eyes I see the delight of thy body and the great gentleness of thy heart. But be merciful, give to the dying *what no other man desires.*"

" Peace be with thee, Odele, daughter of Valdemar, wife of Jürgen Schutte," broke in the old barefooted man. " Fulfil, my daughter, the prayer of the Lord's accursed, show mercy and give him the unneeded rose. The Death Mass was read for him to-day in Church, as is done for lepers, the joiner has prepared his coffin, he is no longer of the living. Be therefore righteous, give to him, as thou wouldſt give to the dead."

And Odele, remembering her prayer to the Virgin Mary and overcoming at laſt the coldness of her heart, grasped the hand of her child and with it caſt the rose to the leper.

And lo ! she saw as it were a vision :

The taint of the diseased ſtanding there before her fell off like large white scales. The gaping sores they left joined up without a scar, in place of the loſt fingers, joint by joint new ones appeared, ulcers grew smooth and were seen no more, the dim eyes regained their luſtre, the skin its clear freshness, the eyebrows their curve, the body its brave and gallant bearing.

She saw that the man she had looked upon as

34

a leper was of the race of brave and splendid humanity, the heart of the Creator had beat high at his birth, the stars had danced a golden measure at his coming into the world.

And Odele, the young wife of Jürgen Schutte, Councillor of the town of Tallinn, and Head of the Hospital of St. John, come from afar, from the land of green beech-woods, fled hurriedly into the garden, confusion and a strange languor in her heart, in her hair a golden bee drunk with honey and ready to sting.

Gerdruta Carponai

I

IN THE SPRING OF 1710, DURING THE
Great Northern War, while the Russians were
besieging Riga, a deadly pestilence called the
Black Death came down from the interior to the
islands, first to Hiiumaa, then to Saaremaa,
thence across the little Sound to Muhu and
finally during the autumn to the lonely island of
Ruhnu.

Many tales are yet told of the coming of the
plague. The fishermen of Hiiumaa were aware
one evening of a strange, forbidding vessel which
had anchored near the harbour of Eltermaa.
They gathered together to discuss the newcomer,
but rowed finally over with provisions. When
they had drawn near, the vessel seemed devoid
of all human life, the deck was empty, the mast
and spars like those on a derelict. They were
about to row back to land, when suddenly a boy
about a foot and a half in height and dressed in
grey, climbed from the hold on to the deck and
jumped straight from the bulwarks into the boat.
Twice they threw the boy into the sea, and twice
he bounced back into the boat, like a grey-scaled
fish. When they reached the shore he dis-

appeared immediately among the hazel-bushes and all they had had time to see of him was that he was dressed in the German ſtyle with a three-cornered hat and a ſtaff in his hand. Then the oldeſt on board the boat clasped his hands and suddenly each began to shiver ; they underſtood : the plague had come to the island. The following day one half of the village of Eltermaa lay dead.

The plague took its victims suddenly ; it germinated in the ground and fell as dew from the sky. People were beset by feverish, poisonous spasms, which caused the blood to boil in their veins. Their heads became roaring furnaces, a numb weakness overcame their limbs, unconsciousness followed, their poisoned blood broke out in blue tumours which covered the neck and armpits. Their faces were diſtorted beyond recognition before death, their senses left them ; within a few hours they died in grievous agony.

Marvellous and terrible things happened ; all was possible. Fiery red cocks sat on gate-poſts and their crow meant death ; whosoever saw them firſt and uttered a word about them, fell and died where he ſtood. God seemed to have forgotten the diſtinctions of class that He Himself had in His wisdom ordained between the Germans and the unfree. The plague chose not, showing no respect for ancient names or noble blood. A name in the book of the Plague betokened death for its owner. Highly-born Councillors of State, estate-owners and knights whose pedigrees stretched to the Crusades, died like the most wretched truck-servants or day-labourers ; the one in his oaken bed, the other on his bundle of straw. At the poorhouse both keepers and inmates died. The former German merchants of Kuresaar fell dead among the ruins of their demolished dwellings, behind the smoke-stacks of which they had sought shelter. Priests sank down in their pulpits while arraigning a generation so deep in sin that its degradation had called down Heaven's punishment ; the bell-ringers died as they tolled the funeral chimes for others. It was plain : God had closed the doors and windows of Heaven, but the gates of Hell stood wide open.

Having sought in vain for shelter in the Holy Sacrament and at the altar of the Church, men began secretly to sacrifice on the stone of Upa and in the sacred grove at Kaarma, where at the foot of a sacred holy mountain ash, human blood had once been spilt to appease Taara. But the old peasant gods were dead or become blind and deaf in their old age. Christ, the only son of God, was helpless, but equally so Taara, the god of peasants.

But at night the little grey man passed from hut to hut, from manor to manor. The charred doors of chimneyless huts opened before him as easily as the brass-clamped portals of the manors, and he touched the sleepers below the heart with the sharp point of his staff.

Summer came, and with it drought and heat, and the plague waxed fiercer. Whole villages were exterminated. The corpses were carried in loads to the bog-pits, piled over one another so that the flaxen tresses of young maidens swept the road as they passed. But soon there were no grave-diggers, and the dead lay as they fell, no one daring to touch them.

The fields were left unploughed, meadows became choked with undergrowth. In the lifeless villages, where the bodies lay unburied, the cattle, left to themselves, ran wild. Cows roamed in the forests, lowing with bursting udders. The spirit of the wolf awoke in homeless dogs ; they attacked the flocks they had been set to herd, or, thinned to the bone, they crept through the villages, wondering whither the masters that fed them had disappeared. The ſtarving swine broke from their ſtyes and satisfied their hunger on the bodies of the plague-ſtricken, lying unblessed by the Church. From their hiding places in the marsh islands and the foreſts of Sõrve and Karja came the wolves, and with the freezing of the Great and Little Sounds the bears left the interior, seeking their prey.

The race of man seemed doomed to perish. Life came to a ſtandſtill with all the common tasks of man, the ploughing, the sowing and reaping, the hunt for game or fish, marriage. It seemed God's purpose to empty the land of man, and bring it to the ſtate that prevailed before man's creation. But the land was far from being a Paradise. It was burned and waſted, and over the waters the Angel of Deſtruction moved.

II

At the time when all was God-forsaken a prieſt of German race lived in one of the coaſtal parishes, called Magnus Carponai and married to Beata von Krämer, of gentle birth, the daughter of a Councillor of State. They had several children, amongſt whom a daughter Gerdruta, nineteen years old, was the eldeſt. As so often with German maidens of noble birth brought up in

the country, Gerdruta Carponai was of healthy
and blooming appearance, over-browned perhaps
in the summers by the sea wind, well propor-
tioned, and with hair the colour of wild nuts
inclining to copper as with her mother's family,
eyes as blue-green gems, a finely modelled bridge
to her delicately chiselled, aristocratic nose.
When she sat beside her mother with proud neck
bent, as befitted a virtuous maiden, in the vicarage pew at church, the noble youths who arrived
on horseback or driving teams of four at the
German service, all gazed in her direction.   One
Sunday, her cousin on her mother's side, Rembert von Rehren, of the manor of Loona and
serving in the garrison at Fort Kuresaar, remained
at the vicarage for the evening.   August had set
in and the dark cherries were ripening.   Rembert
von Rehren seized a ladder, and, climbing into a
tree, began to pelt Gerdruta with ripe cherries.
Gerdruta gathered them in her hands and her
apron ; finally she cast herself down in the grass
below the tree and attempted with her lips to
catch the falling berries, which gleamed like the
ruddiest amber and split asunder with their
ripeness.   Rembert von Rehren was pale as he
descended the ladder ; his eyes could not quit
the blood of cherries on Gerdruta's lips.   Stand-

ing opposite each other they were almost of a
height, ruddy-haired, long-necked members of
the same race. The vicarage garden was moist
and silent : under a lichen-clad cherry-tree they
kissed.

This happened, as legend tells, in August.
The whole winter Gerdruta Carponai prepared
her trousseau, the nuptials were announced for
the beginning of May. But they were stern
times and troubled, and in March the Cossacks
and Tartars attacked and plundered the country
from Kuivaste on Muhu to Sõrve Säär. In
their footsteps came the plague, Rembert von
Rehren being one of the first officers to die in the
garrison of Kuresaar ; he was followed by the
greater part of the garrison.

At the end of June death swept through the
Carponais' parish. It was one of the most fertile
and thickly populated on Saaremaa ; wherefore
the destruction caused by the plague was greater
than elsewhere, the sickness seeking out the most
fertile spots. Carponai set watchmen on the
roads from other parishes, forbidding the entrance
of beggars and strangers to the parish. He
prepared a powder of sulphur and pine resin, with
which he smoked the dwellings ; the thresholds
he sprinkled with vinegar and nitric acid. He

caused bonfires of juniper to be lit round the villages, to be kept alight day and night. The congregation gathered for common prayer at the Church. Nothing was of avail. The plague defied both prayers and nitric acid ; it passed through fire and the smoke of burning juniper.

Carponai continued the fight with the courage of despair. He forced the survivors to drag out the bodies of the dead with boathooks through the windows and convey them to the grave. His wife and the four youngest children died ; for lack of a sexton he climbed the steeple himself and tolled the funeral chimes. He would not surrender ; as long as his feet would bear him, he attended the sick and comforted the dying. His daughter Gerdruta accompanied him, with eyes like blue-green ice, opened wide and cold, her mouth dead and pale. One morning Carponai felt a fierce heat in his blood—it was the plague. He did not doubt for a moment that death was nigh and he commanded his daughter Gerdruta to bury the silver chalice and paten in the ground beside the church. This done, he caused Gerdruta to bring the church registers, writing with nerveless hand in large and painstaking letters *omnes mortui*—all dead.

When Carponai drew his last breath the sun

43

was already high in the sky. Gerdruta covered her father's body with a sheet and, going out, sat down on the lowest step of the stairs ; she understood now that she was alone.

None other created in the same mould as herself existed ; man, God's image, had died out.

A great agony of the soul, deeper than bodily pain, came over her ; she shouted out and then waited. But the silence continued, there was no one else.

Then Gerdruta decided to await death on the threshold of her home. She prayed to be allowed to die, offering voluntarily her youthful limbs, her virgin body to the plague.

But the hours sped by and death came not.

With the coming of evening she remembered suddenly that a one-eyed old woman, nearly ninety years of age, Liiva Ingel, had been alive a few days earlier. She remembered having passed Liiva Ingel's hut and seen smoke curling from the smoke-hole.

Gedruta Carponai felt that God Himself had sent this thought. She set forth immediately, going straight over pasture-lands and bog, and her yearning to see a living human being was so great that it wellnigh stifled her.

44

What mattered it that this being was a bleary-eyed, foul old woman, tottering on the verge of the grave !

Breaking through the laſt hazel-thicket, Gerdruta paused : before her lay a juniper heath with one lonely hut set in its midſt. But the door was shut, likewise the smoke-trap, and no smoke was visible.

Gerdruta tried to persuade herself that the old woman had no fire burning at the time. But on opening the door of the hut, a familiar scene met her gaze : on the bed lay Liiva Ingel, dead of the plague ; her body already cold and in the firſt ſtage of decomposition.

As though ſtruck to the heart, Gerdruta Carponai turned and fled to the great foreſts, no longer knowing what she did. She fled before her own loneliness, heavier to bear than the plague itself.

III

Gerdruta Carponai did not know afterwards how long she had wandered in the wilds and bogs of Saaremaa. It was morning when she reached the seashore, a bright morning, a joy for inſects and human beings alike. But the heart of Gerdruta Carponai ached with loneliness and was heavy with death ; she decided to wait there and die.

She bent down to cast herself upon the beach, when suddenly in the damp sand she became aware of a human footprint.

There was no mistaking it. It was of recent date, the impress of a firm foot, the marks of toes and heel plainly visible, the instep arched. Behind it was a second, a third, a whole line of footprints along the smooth sand, disappearing only over a rise towards the land.

Gerdruta nearly collapsed. A human footprint ! The world was not then empty of men. She was not alone.

And bending lower than ever before even the mightiest in the land, the proud, gentleborn Gerdruta Carponai bowed down and, with eyes brimming over with tears, humbly kissed the footprint of the unknown in the sand.

But the sudden joy proved too strong for her exhausted body, she drooped like a reed, and falling, lay senseless on the sand.

The sun had travelled a long way through the sky and was shining directly over the grey rocks when she awoke. She had slept many hours. She saw that while asleep she had been carried to the water's edge and placed on a heap of nets, a bundle of dry reeds serving as pillow. To the left the shore rose in high rocky cliffs straight from the sea, but close under the cliffs she could see a dozen or so chimneyless huts and drying-poles for nets. The sea was calm, but a hollow booming told of a hidden swell.

Beside her a young man was broiling flatfish between two stones. He was dressed in ordinary peasant attire, wearing a coarse hempen robe kept together by a parti-coloured belt, and no footwear. He was very thin, with long un-combed light hair, eyes light-grey.

Seeing Gerdruta awake, he said in the peasant tongue without leaving his occupation :

" Thou wilt eat ? "

Gerdruta only nodded in reply. The man handed her a fish and she ate. The fish was fresh and fat, but without salt.

" All dead ? " asked the man.

" Dead,—every one," Gerdruta answered in the peasant tongue.

" Here too," the man said.

They sat silent a while, secretly examining each other.

" I am Laes—Kadariku Laes—from yonder hut," said the man finally. " And thou ? "

" Gerdruta Carponai," replied Gerdruta.

47

And even as she spoke she was fully aware that who she might be was as little of account as the white cloud above her that melted in the sun.

The man only stirred the fire and said :

" rom thy dress I saw thee to be a German. But now we are the only living in the whole parish."

" I saw thy footprints in the sand," Gerdruta said.

The man glanced at his sunburned brown feet and nodded.

" I went to carry water from the spring," he said.

Having finished their meal they set out for the cliffs.

Evening was already nigh.

On the summit of the cliffs dark-coloured late strawberries grew beneath the junipers that had been gnawed all over by sheep, though berrying time was long over.

They bent down to pick them, gave them to one another and ate.

The berries had a spiced and perfumed flavour. They ate a long time, like children, among the juniper bushes.

The setting sun, sinking towards the distant, invisible Ojumaa, shone in their faces, but there was no need for them to close their eyes against it. The sun floated in banks of warm grey mist, emitting no rays.

"What is it that boom?" asked Gerdruta.

"There are other cliffs under the water," Laes explained. "One must pour ale and vodka into the sea there, otherwise there will be no luck in fishing."

They sat on the cliff's edge, sated with berries. Neither asked what was to follow. Beneath them was the cliff of slate, a hundred feet in height.

But for Gerdruta Carponai it was as though she had been born in a world altogether new.

It was a world she had never before visited. As in the former, here were air, land and sea, but the only mortals were they two, Kadariku Laes and Gerdruta Carponai.

The seagulls hovered over the water, with wings black in the shadow, a humming and murmuring arose from the grass. Everything in nature continued to live. But they two were the only human beings left.

There were no longer slaves or free; German or peasant, class or station. All that man had built up during the centuries had gone.

Under a thick cluster of juniper quite close to

them, a viper bathed in the failing sunshine. Laes noticed it at the same time as Gerdruta and in the same instant he had cut off a branch, split it at one end and caught the viper's head in it as in a vice.

Gerdruta saw the snake writhing at the end of the stick, yellow stomached, black stripes along its back, the forked tongue playing from its mouth.

" Rästik,"[1] Laes said, and lifted it high into the air.

He did not kill it, however; instead he cast it away, far behind him.

" The grain stops growing if a snake is killed," he explained his action.

But as Laes cast the snake from him it was as though Gerdruta saw him for the first time, saw his youthful frame, thin with starvation, the fine firm line of his jaw and beneath it a horizontal scar with even edges as though from a blow with a knife,—his nose, with wide nostrils, high and straight between his eyes, his hands, which in their strength resembled sledge-hammers. Neither the hempen robe nor the effects of hunger could hide the youthful strength of his body.

---

[1] Estonian for viper, or adder.

Its every movement was swift, to the purpose and economical of strength.

At the same time she became aware that Laes was deep in like contemplation of herself. As he looked on her she felt herself flushing red. Almost at the same moment they turned away in opposite directions.

After that they looked at each other no more. They descended from the cliffs to the shore again. The surface of the rock was dotted with beds of rock-crystal, like the petrified nests of prehistoric birds. The sea was brightly smooth, its bottom paved with flat layers of rock like a floor.

There, on the deserted shore, in a country empty of human inhabitants, it came to both at once. Death rose to their brains as a mighty intoxication. They were drunk with it as with strong drink. Their youthful healthy bodies yearned unknowing each for the other, to create new life on the wasted earth. All the desolation they had seen burned in their brains, arousing in them a strange passion.

There were only they two.

The sun had set when they returned to the hut of Laes. Laes, the fisher, opened the door and the highly-born Gerdruta Carponai entered. And in their fierce embrace on the bed of straw, their horror of death mingled with the yearning for life of generations yet to come. The world was empty and to these two fell the duty of repeopling it, and they were as alone as the two first human beings.

IV

This is the tale of Gerdruta Carponai, during the year of the Black Death of Saaremaa.

As may be seen from the church registers for the time of the Great Northern War, the five sons of Kadariku Laes were baptized seven years later at midsummer, all at the same time. Their mother, Gerdruta Carponai, daughter of the former vicar of the parish, the worthy Magnus Carponai, and of his gentle-born wife, Beata von Krämer, had on the other hand to atone for her sin by sitting three Sundays following on the bench for immodest women in her father's church, for all to see. Thus, the stern and uncompromising vicar of that time, Heinrich Bürger has with his own hand written in the church register : " —*hat auf dem berüchtigten Hurenschemel ihre Sedes halten müssen.*"

Whosoever wishes, may even to-day see this bench among the other lumber of the church : a low, wooden bench, fenced in like a pen.

After Gerdruta Carponai had thus publicly atoned for her sins in the sight of the whole congregation and received absolution at the altar, she was given in Chriſtian wedlock to Kadariku Laes and taken again into the fold of the Church. From the mouth of the people one may hear that the whole present population of the parish had this couple to thank for its being, according to which they have increased within two centuries in far more wondrous measure than the children of Israel in Egypt.

Of the later phases of Gerdruta Carponai's life nothing is known. She disappeared from the sight of men as a ſtone sinks in a bog, disappeared for ever in the low caſte of her husband, into an alien people, unacknowledged by her own family or caſte. Her children were fishers and slaves. But she had lived through a world hidden since the days of Paradise from men : a world without grades of value, without caſte or class, without the many-coloured tinsels of man's devising, a world with two lovers dwelling in it alone.

A Bathsheba of Saaremaa

FROM THE TIME OF NICOLAI I

KUIGU ANTS, the manor blacksmith.
VIIU, HIS wife.
OLD-KAI, his mother.

(*A threshing-barn, drying-poles suspended from the
roof, floor of stamped earth, on the right a large
stove the upper part of which extends over an
open hearth, on which is a fire burning under
a cauldron suspended from a hook, before the
fire a three-legged, iron-edged stand for pird,[1]
in the corner to the left a huge bed, under the
window a weaving-loom and spinning wheel.
A trap-door in the floor leading to the cellar.
It is evening. Viiu, a high-bosomed, bright-
eyed young woman, comes in bearing a bucket,
with frock turned up almost to the knee.*)

OLD-KAI (*a blear-eyed, bent woman, leans over
from the top of the large stove*). I believe I heard
the door—I could feel the draught even here—
is that Viiu. . . ? Viiu.

VIIU. What is the matter now ?

OLD-KAI. Were you in the cowshed ?

---

[1] *Thin strips of wood, used as torches or candles by peasants in
hours of darkness.*

VIIU. Taking mash to the cows—if you don't believe me, here's the bucket.

OLD-KAI. I believe you—of course I believe you. . . . I suppose there's right royal weather outside ?

VIIU. Snowing to choke up the yard—I was up to my knees in snow.

OLD-KAI. There'll be drifts on the highway, too. . . . (*Cautiously.*) I suppose you didn't go as far as the fork of the roads ?

VIIU (*bends down over a tub, which she begins to clean*). Why should I have gone there ?

OLD-KAI. Ah, that's it, what should you have had to do there. (*Begins to climb down from the top of the oven.*)

VIIU. Bless us, Granny—whither away ?

OLD-KAI. Let me go—I will go and see.

VIIU. For God's sake, don't go. You will fall on your face in the snow.

OLD-KAI. Let me go—my whole body is so restless for Ants' sake.

VIIU (*quickly*). It is of no use, there is no sign of any one yet.

OLD-KAI. How do you know ?

VIIU. Because I went to look.

OLD-KAI. You should have said so before— would the truth cost you a half kopek. I believe even your heart is beating for the safety of your husband.

VIIU. Granny, listen—what do you believe—why does Ants delay so ?

OLD-KAI. God knows . . . whether for the best or for the worst—perhaps they will yet release him at the examination and not take him for a soldier.

VIIU (*drawing out her words*). Do you think so, Granny ?

OLD-KAI. Do I know—he has the baron's letter with him. He will not be taken against the baron's will.

VIIU (*rising rapidly*). Yes—he has the baron's letter—won't you come and eat, Granny.

OLD-KAI. I don't know—whether I can swallow anything this evening.

VIIU. I will lay out the pickled sprats ready—and pour the sour milk into the bowl.

OLD-KAI. I haven't the peace of mind to eat. Did you hear anything ?

VIIU (*in alarm*). I wasn't listening.

OLD-KAI. You were sitting again with your ear on a level with the window.

VIIU. Granny, listen, if they take Ants for a soldier—will they really keep him for five-and-twenty years ?

OLD-KAI. The Czar is satisfied with no less.

VIIU (*softly*). But then he will be an old man.

OLD-KAI. What . . . ?

VIIU. He will be an old man when he returns, I said.

OLD-KAI. Old, of course—as though the sap had been let run dry from a tree, fit for the scrap-heap. And no good for work on the land any longer—a sword is not a ploughshare, though they are made of the same iron. Their fingers no longer bend to a scythe. Lazy good-for-nothings they learn to be, only fit to sit in the taverns. They say some even forget their language, begin to jabber Russian—kakpusivai—karasoo [1]—some forget how to talk at all. Is it any wonder that the young men hide in the marshes when ordered to the examinations? But where are you to hide on an island, with the sea always before you?

VIIU. What will become of me? A living man's widow. Married and not married.

OLD-KAI. You?—a place will always be found for you. You might go back as housemaid to the manor—that is still in your blood—these

[1] *Estonian peasants' rendering of Russian greetings : " How do you do ? ", " Very well."*

57

earthen floors are not for the hem of your dress.

VIIU. Don't chatter nonsense, old woman.

OLD-KAI. As though I didn't know—your hands are too fine for these lowly tasks. . . . Oh, you do everything, yes, but with uplifted nose and skirts held high. . . . If you even had a child—you could nurse and hush that. . . . Ants would not have been wanted for a soldier then—the Crown seldom bothers about men with a family to keep. . . . But no—married over a year, and still as thin as a hop-pole.

VIIU. That's right, begin scolding again.

OLD-KAI. What is a childless woman good for ? —like a field laying fallow. Too much spare time—begins to brood on all kinds of foolishness.

VIIU. Be silent at once. . . . Living there on the top of the stove, like an owl in the corner of a garret—thinking you see and know everything. I am as good as anyone else.

OLD-KAI. Perhaps something in the style I said, after all. . . . Listen, Viiu.

VIIU. Leave me alone—I have not said a word.

OLD-KAI. Does Ants know ?

VIIU (*begins to wash the earthenware dishes with great clatter*).

OLD-KAI. What were you doing at the manor this morning ?

VIIU. What was I doing ?—my turn at the cattlesheds.

OLD-KAI. Since when have you had a turn with the cattle ?—you didn't do it at first.

VIIU. Since laſt month—haven't you known ?

OLD-KAI. Who takes the trouble to tell me anything now ?—better would it be to be deaf and dumb as a clod of earth. But I am not blind yet, though I crouch on the oven.

VIIU. What are you driving at . . . ?

OLD-KAI. I say only that a cat's eyes see in the dark.

VIIU (*pauses—liſtens*). Ui-ih. Good God.

OLD-KAI. What are you shrieking at ?—you made even my heart jump into my throat.

VIIU. Wasn't it like the scrape of a sleigh—liſten—the runners grating on the snow—the horse's hoofs beating the soft drifts—if Ants were to come now . . . I daren't liſten—I shall cover my head—I shall get into my bed and cover my ears—say that I'm asleep, that I have fallen ill, that I am dead—anything.

OLD-KAI. Stop it now—it drove paſt—towards the church—liſten Viiu—don't tremble so—take a drink of water—look at her, trembling all over her body.

VIIU. Uh-ih, what if he came now ?

OLD-KAI. Be silent, no one is coming. I would never have believed that you could have fallen into such agony over Ants.

VIIU. Leave me in peace, Granny.

OLD-KAI. Don't, my good woman, be so distressed—Ants has the baron's letter.

VIIU (*rising coldly*). You also believe in the baron's letter, as though God Father had written it.

OLD-KAI. How did it happen with the letter —what if you were to tell me about it.

VIIU. You have heard it once already.

OLD-KAI. I have such poor hearing—half of what is told me falls by the wayside. Did you see the baron himself?

VIIU. Yes.

OLD-KAI (*cautiously feeling her way*). Was he alone in the room?

VIIU. Yes, or I don't quite remember—wait— perhaps the gracious mistress was there too.

OLD-KAI. What was the mistress doing there?

VIIU. What do gracious mistresses do?—sit about with their hands crossed.

OLD-KAI. Don't wriggle out of it—there was no mistress in the room.

VIIU. You seem to know more about it than I do.

OLD-KAI. And the baron promised to write

60

to the Army people, what? That they should not take Ants for a soldier? That he has an old mother, tottering on the verge of her grave? That there are others of the baron's tenants—lazy rascals, wastrels—let them go. Everybody looks the same in Government shoddy—like herrings —pile them any way in a barrel. Though a whole dozen were killed, no one would pity them, or think of them as human beings. Only when you see them in their own clothes can you know that they have land and property, wives and mothers. . . . Did the baron promise to write it all?

VIIU (*occupied at the table*). Granny—you have not eaten a morsel—the potatoes are untouched.

OLD-KAI. Don't confuse me, I want no more, not even if you offered me good fat bacon. . . . I want to know, did the baron write it?

VIIU. I suppose he wrote it then.

OLD-KAI. What—suppose. Don't you know for certain? You went yourself to beg him.

VIIU. Have I read the letter?

OLD-KAI. Did you ask him? Did you beg as for your life? Were you on your knees?— answer——

VIIU. Now you may ask like a priest at confession, but I refuse to answer a word.

OLD-KAI.   Do you want to know what Ants
still possesses—shall I tell you?   Ants has a
young wife, who fawns before the gentry.

VIIU.   Granny—I—I . . .

OLD-KAI.   Claws off, wildcat.   (*A silence.* VIIU
*occupies herself restlessly around the room, treads
the spinning-wheel, rises, adjusts the cloth in the
loom, stops and listens.*)

VIIU.   Aren't you going to bed, Granny?

OLD-KAI.   No.

VIIU.   Do you want anything to eat?—or shall
I clear the table?

OLD-KAI.   No—take it all away.

VIIU.   What do you want then—you might
get on to the stove.   It is warmer there.

OLD-KAI.   Does it worry you if I sit here?

VIIU.   What are you looking at me for?

OLD-KAI.   A cat may look at a king.

VIIU.   Ants will be here no earlier, even if you
wait for him.

OLD-KAI.   Perhaps he is no longer in any hurry.

VIIU (*sharply*).   What do you mean by
that . . . ?

OLD-KAI.   Only that Ants will surely be taken.

VIIU.   How do you know—where . . . ?

OLD-KAI.   There was something else in the
letter.

VIIU. What—do you know?

OLD-KAI. Don't you know too . . . ? Well, why don't you answer? A person can know a great deal more than is shouted in his ear.

VIIU (*does not answer*).

OLD-KAI. Shall I say it—the letter ran: " Take Ants for a soldier." Wasn't it so?

VIIU. Now he is coming, the gelding snorted —Oh God !—I shall run down into the cellar— I can't see it.

OLD-KAI (*rising*). Why does he arrive so wildly, what was that crash—he has snapped off his shafts against the gate-posts, for sure.

ANTS (*throws open the door, in a short sheepskin coat, covered from head to foot with snow, a metal badge with a number on his breast. A dark, smoothly-shaven face, clipped moustache, eyes deep in his head*). Evening—evening, I say—does no one answer?

OLD-KAI. Good evening, my boy.

ANTS (*discarding his coat*). Evening, Viiu— come out where I can see you, do you see what glitters on this boy's chest ?—tinkles like a sleigh-bell, tirilil, tirilil.

OLD KAI. What is it, my boy—a medal?

ANTS. A shining medal like on any great German. Now I am a gentleman too and can

63

live as though each day were the last. To-day
we eat, drink and make merry, kiss the mouth
of a pretty girl—to-morrow before the cannon's
mouth, begging : Ho, comrade there, let's have
a couple of pounds of metal through this little
machine that ticks in our breasts.

OLD-KAI. You have sat in Luuguse tavern
on your way home, my boy.

ANTS. One can be drunk on a day like this,
without a drop of spirits on the tongue. Everything goes to the head—even to breathe makes
one faint. Well, Viiu, come here.

VIIU (*approaches him unwillingly*).

ANTS. Come on, Viiu—sit here, press the
knee of a Government servant, let us hug each
other before the end—hug tighter—so. . . .
Did I hurt you ? was I too rough ?—I have not
a baron's hands—these paws were never washed
in milk, but have grown hard grasping the sledge-
hammer. Perhaps they will smoothen now,
holding a gun.

OLD-KAI (*weeping*). Oh, that they should have
taken you, Ants—there will be no one to close
my eyes when I die.

ANTS. Men hale and hearty cannot be left to
soften in their beds. Have you any vodka at
home, Viiu ?

64

VIIU. None.

ANTS. Why are you so downhearted . . . shall you miss me ? You will be left a widow, but with no hope of a new husband—even from afar I shall hold you. Shall you miss me, Viiu ?

VIIU (*hides her face, weeping*).

ANTS (*softly*). A little, anyhow—I don't ask for much. I shall remember over there, never fear—how you used to come and crouch at the door of the smithy, and the sparks flying—how the iron bent and the hammer fell. . . . No vodka ? Never mind, we can drink pure water, get drunk on that—mother mine, liften.

OLD-KAI. What now, my boy ?

ANTS. Why have you never held evening prayers ? We are all sinners. We can ftill begin. Where is the Bible, Viiu, where is the Bible ?

VIIU. Why do you want it ?

ANTS. You will see. Where is it ?

VIIU. On the shelf there.

ANTS. Give it here—look what an obedient wife I have. . . . And young—eyes shining like wild berries.

OLD-KAI. What are you going to do, my son ?

ANTS. Read the Bible to you, the word of God as nourishment for your souls, as the Prieft says.

Or—Viiu can read it—she has a clear voice, like a bell. I would like to hear of King David— where is there about him ?

VIIU (*turns the pages with trembling fingers— nearly drops the Bible*). Don't—know.

ANTS. You book-learned—don't you know your Bible ? Mother, do you know ?

OLD-KAI. What place do you . . . ?

ANTS. I want to hear how King David loved another man's wife—that Bathsheba.

OLD-KAI. Isn't it in the second Book of Samuel ?

VIIU (*searching the Bible*). I can't find it.

ANTS. Give it here—I shall look for it. Here —there it is, read it.

VIIU. I can't see here—my eyes are too weak.

ANTS (*replaces the old taper with a new*). Now . . . (*with emphasis*) Read, Viiu.

VIIU (*brokenly, swallowing the words*). " And it came to pass after the year was expired, at the time when Kings go forth to battle, that David sent Joab and his servants with him and all Israel; and they destroyed the children of Ammon and besieged Rabbah. But David tarried still at Jerusalem. And it came to pass in an evening-tide, that David arose from his bed and walked upon the roof of the King's house ; and from the roof he saw a woman washing herself, and the woman was very beautiful to look upon. And David sent and inquired after the woman. And one said, Is not this Bathsheba, the daughter of Eliam, the wife of Uriah the Hittite ? " (*breaks out crying*).

ANTS (*takes the book*). Now I shall read a few more verses. " And it came to pass in the morning, that David wrote a letter to Joab and sent it by the hand of Uriah. And he wrote in the letter saying, Set ye Uriah in the forefront of the hotteſt battle, and retire ye from him that he may be smitten and die." (*Closes the book.*) Viiu, when you came to-day from the baron's, did you know what was in the letter ?

VIIU (*in great agony*). O God ! O God !

ANTS. Did you not suspeᴄt it ?

VIIU. I can't—I can't . . .

ANTS. In the name of God, answer.

VIIU (*softly*). I suspeᴄted it.

ANTS. There, now—I knew it. . . . Speak to me now as to a Prieſt. Confess your sins. Begin. What happened at the baron's to-day ?

VIIU. The baron—was—alone. I said : Ants has received the command to go to the muſtering. The baron came, took me by the chin : And you will be left alone, he said. He went to his table, whiſtling : You will be left

67

alone, he said again. He came towards me;
Do you know that twenty-five years is a long
time. . . . Spare him, I said, write a few words
and Ants will not be taken. Oh, you will be
looked after, he said, and laughed. I . . .
laughed also. . . . I wanted to beg, to pray,
but only laughter would come to my lips. You
are as beautiful as ever, he said. And then he
kissed me. . . .

ANTS. And you . . .

VIIU. I pushed him away with my hand—
laughed. You would like better days again, he
said. Have mercy on Ants, I said. The baron
went and wrote quickly on a paper, sealed the
letter. I felt a ſtab in my heart and asked what
he had written. The letter is to see that you will
not have a bad time for twenty-five years, he said.
Then I came home and gave the letter to Ants.

ANTS. And said nothing to me, woman?

VIIU. I said nothing.

ANTS. You let me go in the belief that the
letter was a plea for my freedom?

VIIU. Yes . . . have mercy. . . .

ANTS. Don't come near me, or . . . Don't
touch me or I won't answer for what I do . . .
(*sinks on to a bench, broken in soul*). Bathsheba, a
poor man's only lamb !

The Wedding

A HUNDRED YEARS AGO A WED-
ding was being celebrated on a Saaremaa
farm. In the middle of the room sat the bride,
so that all might see her heated young face ;
the cap newly fastened to her hair and to which
she was as yet unused, compelled her to hold
her head well back, but also otherwise, she hardly
looked the type to bow her head overmuch.
Her hands she kept on her lap on her apron
which was just being " patched " : the guests
filed by with copper or silver coins in their hands
and threw these into the apron. She thanked
them and laughed—seeming but to wait for the
opportunity in order to give rein to the boundless
mirth within her. When the money had been
put away, one of the guests seized a boy about
five years of age from the ring standing round
the bride and set him on her knee for her infant.
Jokes and innuendoes rained on her from all
sides, grave prophetic hopes and bold quips,
sufficient to drive the blood time and again to
the bride's cheeks.

Despite the courage and sincerity of her char-
acter, confusion finally seized her and she lifted
the boy to the floor ; she felt hot, the head-dress

weighed on her temples, a desire to leave the room awoke in her. Hardly noticed, she drew aside, the cooks beginning at the moment to wipe the tables, ſtriking them with loud knocks to solicit contributions. The violins were being tuned in the corner. She edged nearer and nearer the open door and at laſt slipped through it. In the village lane, where geese waddled with their brown-coated young, she almoſt broke into a run before she reached the well. No one noticed her disappearance but the bridegroom, who all the time had kept his eyes on her and now set off after her.

He found his newly-wedded wife on the ledge of the well, bowed down in an attempt to hoiſt the bucket. A fence and a cluſter of hop-bushes sheltered them from the house. Hearing foot-ſteps, she turned as though caught in some evil deed. " It was so hot," she said, as though begging for his forgiveness. But the bridegroom ſtood holding the well-poſt, unhurriedly gazing at his bride—and then, as though by some silent agreement, she sat herself down on the cover of the well, in the cracks of which the grass grew. " Let us ſtay here a while," she begged. The bridegroom nodded his head without removing his gaze from her face, and to both came a feeling of mingled pleasure and guilt, as though without permission they grasped something belonging by right to others.

The bride dipped her hand in the well-trough, which was split at one end. At the other end, where the water had collected, two or three bees were swimming, fallen into the water in an attempt to drink. She stretched out her finger and the bees crawled in a single file along it to safety. They began to flutter their wings rapidly and to rub them with their legs, their hind-legs swiftly wiping their bodies covered with fine hairs ; they dragged their legs along her finger, leaving long tracks of moisture. Suddenly, one crawled higher and disappeared into her sleeve.

" It will sting thee," the young man cried with a sudden movement.

But the girl stretched her arm downwards and shook the bee into the grass, her face glowing with pleasure at the man's concern.

Then both turned to listen to the dance-music as the shrill notes of violins and bagpipes came from the bride's home. " They are searching for us," the girl whispered, and the young man nodded. They looked away from the lane and from the house, from the chimney of which arose the smoke of festal cooking, towards the plain before them, to where an early summer sun was setting in a cloudless sky. The purple rye-fields formed an obtuse angle with the sky and behind them the west glowed with promise of the coming harvest, as though it were written there in the heavens that the fields should give back their fruits tenfold. Behind the fence stretched the grazing-ground, dear to them in its barrenness because of its promise of work also for them. Farther back, the church stood erect—the only rising point on the plain—ruling the neighbourhood, visible from whatever point men looked.

The summer air was alive with midges, dancing everywhere. The bride sitting on the edge of the well felt them blindly strike against her face ; she waved them away with a branch she had picked up, but even then they forced their way into her ears, her mouth and her eyes. A sudden smarting in one eye, as though it had been stung, made her lift her hand to rub it.

" A midge flew into my eye," she said.

" Don't rub it—I will take it out," the bride-groom answered hurriedly.

He had no need to bend down ; standing opposite each other they were almost of a height, their eyes meeting. The man drew down the lid of her eye slightly, so that he could see the insect as a tiny black object on its inner surface. He brought his face still nearer, intending to remove it with his tongue, and in this position he saw what earlier had escaped him: the fine veins covering the white of her eye, the tiny freckles on her nose, spreading towards her cheeks. It was all beautiful to him and his thoughts turned to his coming happiness. The girl knew, but continued to look openly at him, with no hint of confusion, ready to surrender, but without excitement, with calm, trusting eyes.

" Let us go in," she said taking his hand in hers.

As they passed within they became aware of a bent man approaching along the lane from the highway. He moved slowly, dragging his steps. To the eyes of both he moved as one bidden to a funeral, not as a wedding guest.

" It is the oldest bailiff of the manor," the bridegroom remarked. " Do thou set ale before him."

The girl looked at him half in wonder, the same thought having just awoke in her, that none but she herself should bring the welcoming tankard to this last guest.

She took a tankard with decorative carvings along its wooden sides and went to an adjoining building, but at the door she glanced instinctively back. The room seemed brighter to her than usual, and she could see that the faces of all who stood near the back window were drenched with the red glow of the sunset. Each time a couple danced past the window they swam for a time in a ruddy cloud. The new guest stood in the shadow.

The bride fumbled in the dark room for the tap of the ale-barrel, when suddenly she started. The buzz of the rejoicing guests had suddenly altered its key—the whole house seemed suddenly to draw in its breath and sigh. . . . The bride's fingers clung uncertainly to the tankard, something heavy seemed to descend over her— a sudden desire to sit on the flour-bin and weep came over her—why, she could not have said, but she was afraid to go back to the house.

With the foaming tankard in her hand she opened the door of the bridal room, but stopped on the threshold so that ale dripped from the tankard to the floor. Her glance sped inquiringly round the room, but all eyes turned away before its question, seeking the floor. Only a vague sense of calamity remained, a hidden oppression seemed to bring the roof lower over their heads, the strings of the violins were mute as though suddenly ſtiffened. Many of the women began to weep, the men gazed darkly before them. She sought her mother with her eyes—the good woman's face was hidden by a shawl—her father —his eyes fixed to the floor—her husband . . . from him at laſt she caught a glance, but only for a moment, then his eyes, too, avoided hers.

At the same time her father rose grown of a sudden old, his limbs hanging loosely as though crushed, all making way as before a great sorrow —he went towards an inner room—the light faded from his face. She felt that she muſt follow him, but in going she seemed to be walking through an empty chamber—she looked at no one, knowing that at this moment all others were but speĉtators, and their curiosity and pity hurt her. She lifted up her head so that her high headgear almoſt swept the low ceiling. But passing her mother she softened, her eyes begged her mother to follow her, and obediently her mother rose, timidly, bathed in tears.

The door closed behind them.

" Say nothing," her mother said pleadingly to her father.

" How childish of mother to say that," the girl thought, but underſtood at once that only love had diĉtated the words.

But she felt that the blow was coming. . . .

" Thou art ordered to the manor for the night, my girl," her father said abruptly.

She opened her eyes, the blow had fallen— she was astounded to find herself still alive. A strong sense of resistance awoke in her.

" I am bidden there, but I have not gone yet," she burst out sharply as though striking with a hammer at an invisible nail.

" Here there is no mercy ; such is the justice of the gentry," her father answered sombrely.

She felt her father's words like weights on her proudly-lifted neck, forcing her to bow down. But she resisted still.

" Word is to be sent that no one comes from this house," she said.

Her father listened as to the speech of a child.

" What would it help us ?   They would drive us to the highway."

" Then we can beg, the whole crowd of us."

" And you would be taken by force in any case."

She felt how the fetters around her were drawn tighter, but still she refused to yield.

" Let us go to the judge," she said.

" To meet the same gentry there.   The Czar is high, God in His sky."

" Mother—and thou ? " she questioned.

" Thou art neither the first nor the last, my child," her mother said between her tears.

She looked helplessly at them, divining that both had already surrendered, that neither intended resistance.

" Beg Jaan to come here," she said.

At the approach of the bridegroom she felt ashamed, as though guilty of some sin.

" Couldst thou take me back—after that ? " she whispered.

" It is that I cannot say," the bridegroom replied.

" I would take thee back, but I don't know whether I should feel to you the same," he added hurriedly in explanation.

" That is so—naturally," the bride humbly answered. " Though many others have gone and have come back," she added, in a tone conveying that she only half believed her own words.

" Others may go and come back, but one of thy kind does not come back," the man answered with weight.

" Canst thou say what I should do ? " she asked in agony.

" I know not yet myself," the man replied.

77

" It is not so much to me whether thou takeſt me back again, as whether thou remaineſt the same," the girl said as though this thought had filled her all the time and now only had found expression in words.

The girl looked at the man, but a miſt seemed to divide them and she was compelled to fumble for his hand as though at leaſt to feel his presence. All at once, it seemed to her that in the eyes looking at her through the miſt something had gleamed—had he found a way out ? she wondered. The hand tightly clenching her own was hot and trembled, as though the blood coursed fitfully and irregularly through it. She felt it twitch and an unseen ſtrength flow like a ſtream from it into her own veins. Something was born in the miſt between them, something waxed—shapeless, terrible. . . . The eyes seemed to ask something of her, they gazed in command at her —silently, without words they demanded something of her. . . . She tried to underſtand what the man wanted, but the miſt was before her, she ſtrained every faculty, seemed to be torn from herself and to be drawn up into those eyes . . . she began to tremble . . . the miſt before her eyes turned red. Something not to be defined united them at the moment—something neither love nor hate—but a thought born simultaneously in them both.

Suddenly, the man bent forward, his lips moving, and she read on them a question :

" Couldst thou dare ? "

" I dare," she answered as silently.

As though the mist had suddenly dissolved they saw each other in a bright light, a clear resolve in the eyes of both.

" But wouldst thou follow me to hard labour in Siberia ? " the girl asked.

" I will follow wherever thou art taken."

" But with what shall I . . ." the girl said, breaking off her words.

" With this," the man replied cautiously, drawing the knife from his belt.

They gazed coldly at each other, not as newly-wedded, but as companions in crime, in whom the criminal's doubt and mutual hate even now took root.

Suddenly the man melted.

" Our wedding-night," he exclaimed.

The girl started, but did not budge. And both understood that not on a midsummer night such as this, bright and perfume-laden, would it come to them, but dark and forbidding fall over them in the gleam of a convict's hut in Siberia.

Ingel

INGEL, THE WET NURSE FROM
Sõrve, sat with a child in her lap on the steps.
The Sõrve stocking-cap was askew over one ear,
the many-coloured tassel nodded at each movement of her head—a preposterous, coquettish
cap, invented in some hour of exuberant, over-
flowing merriment. The frock in the Sõrve
fashion reached in heavy folds to her armpits,
hiding the shape of her body beneath its clumsy
lines, white and red lines running side by side
over a background of solemn black.

Ingel was a powerfully built, high-bosomed
woman of gentle, pleasing countenance, her open
features showing in their modelling an admix-
ture of blood from the island Swedes. She sat
inert, her head drooping somewhat, her eyes half-
closed, almost asleep from the mingled effects of
the sunshine and the child suckling evenly at
her breast. A kind of vegetative peace emanated
from her, as from a large, beautiful plant, whose
leaves hang in the oppressive heat.

Smoothly, slowly, Estonian strength flowed
from her into a child of alien blood. Her blood
coursed in the child's veins, forming new cells,
new nerves, sinews, muscles. It flowed to the

child's brain, to the soft membranes on which no thought as yet had left its mark. She allowed her healthy blood, the whole of her unused funds of strength to flow into the delicate offshoot of another race, the blood of which had become thin in the course of generations.

Not one bitter thought, no accusation, none of the instinctive hatred of the slave, mingled with the milk with which she nurtured the child. She was as peaceful and fruit-giving as the earth itself, which recks not for whom its fruit grows, whether for master or for slave. No thought of whom she might be bringing up, perhaps a new tyrant for her race, lived in her. It never occurred to her that the tiny hand might at one time be lifted to strike.

The child hardly awoke for its meal, suckling with closed eyes the meal offered it. Gravely calm, it was as sure of its right to possess as a monarch, like all children for whom the lack of food is an unknown experience. Its tiny, rosy features were almost hidden among the tapes and laces squandered on its attire, it was wrapped in a coverlet of silk and linen swaddling-bands, a masterpiece of knitting, a cap of finest lace hid the thin growth of hair on its head. A full consciousness of all this comfort and care dwelt in

its eight-month head ; knowing that its slightest
desire would be satisfied, there was no need for
it to cry or fret. Especially was the nurse its
undisputed property, existing solely for its needs,
a being of no importance otherwise. It knew
that the nurse would not cry out though gripped
by the hair, even with the full strength of its tiny
hand ; the nurse would not dare to move though
it plunged the four new teeth into her breast.

The nurse removed the child carefully from
her breast to her lap, fastening her white garment
with a metal clasp. A slight shiver passed through
her limbs as though the wind had breathed on
her. Perhaps she had slumbered and a bee
had stung her in her sleep, perhaps a cloud had
passed over the sun. She awoke to complete
consciousness, the soul returning to her eyes,
hitherto empty of all thought.

Her employers had departed on a week's
visit to a neighbouring parish. One could ob-
serve it from all that occurred around her : the
valet lording it everywhere and playing the master,
scolding the servants and flirting with the housemaid. The old gardener was engaged in clip-
ping the hawthorn hedge to a level wall of green,
but paused every now and then in his work to
take snuff. Even the flag drooped at half-mast,

a sign of the absence of the family. The very garden seemed to have regained its freedom, the bees were humming twice as loudly, the songbirds knew no fear.

Ingel could not understand the strange feeling of faintness below her heart. As though something gnawed there with little, sharp teeth. And as though a hole grew there, an increasing emptiness.

It was neither hunger nor thirst, but resembled both. Some instinct, an uncertain desire seemed to awake in her being. A sense of drought and weakness possessed her whole body, awakening a wish to run quickly to the spring and there dip her head, her mouth, temples and neck in its icy water. The sense of emptiness grew without ceasing and was as a hunger that consumed not only her body but every thought.

Something had been taken from her, from both body and soul, almost as though an arm had been hacked off, or an eye pierced, so helpless and painful was her state of mind. Some tiny portion of her was missing. And now the whole of her being yearned towards this missing part, drawn strongly to it. She sat immovably in her place, and yet it seemed as though she ran and ran, seeking the tiny, lost portion of her being.

It availed nothing that she was replete with food, warm and comfortable. The feeling of emptiness refused to respond to these. She was ill in spite of them. Her senses had become unnaturally sharpened ; it seemed to her that she heard the piping of a child from the shore at Sõrve ; its cry was there in every sound around her, in the mournful chirrup of the rain-bird, in the murmur of the limes.

Then, of a sudden, she remembered the cat at home, whose kittens her father had drowned. She remembered how it crawled with belly on the ground, mewing mournfully, seeking its young. The sparrow, too, whose neſt was emptied by a hawk, how it chirped on the eaves, and fluttered round its neſt, calling its young with ſtrange, throaty notes.

Blood called even among animals. And she was forbidden a single visit to her child by the gracious lady. Only once had she escaped there secretly, at the risk of the whip, running the whole diſtance as though for her life, glancing back over her shoulder to see whether she was pursued. Merciful God, how they had played with the child ; tears of laughter rose to her eyes at the thought. She had pretended to be a dog and to bite the child : the bow-wow comes, bow-wow. . . . And then she had taken the child's foot or hand in her mouth and fondled it gently with her teeth.   The child had screamed with mirth, laughing its firſt laugh, a queer little crow like that of a young cock, and drawing its legs and arms into a knot, had endeavoured again to reach her mouth with its toes.

Would the child ſtill suckle at her breaſt ? She became hot at the thought, the blood seeming to thicken in her head.   If only she might try once, only one little time, she would bear the parting for even a whole year to come.   If only she might once give herself to her own child, become one with it, body and soul, feel blood unite with blood. . . .

"Tiiu—come here."

Tiiu came running towards her.

"Tiiu—go and fetch my son, for a little while only, doſt thou hear."

"Not I, the miſtress might hear of it."

"The miſtress will not be here for a week. Doſt expeƈt the news will carry to another parish ? "

"The others might tell . . ."

"Not they—we shall take it to the nursery. Tiiu, liſten, I will give thee this silver clasp."

Ingel began to unfaſten the little silver ring

at her breaſt. The girl swung on her toes before her, watching Ingel's fingers.

"When thy time for confirmation comes, I will give silk for thy hood, as sure as I live."

"Mottled silk?"

"And therewith silver lace—go now as quickly as thou canſt."

"Well, if thou beareſt the whole blame. Say that thou broughteſt it thyself."

The girl sprang on her errand, climbed like a cat over the garden wall and disappeared into the fields. Ingel went to the nursery and laid the child she bore in her arms in a cradle lined with blue silk, whose eiderdown feathers sank at the lighteſt touch.

What if the child should refuse her breaſt; What if it closed its chubby lips and turned away? Perhaps she would be a ſtranger to it.

Or—what if it had died of lack of care and unsuitable food. No one would breathe a word to her; not until much later when the ſtranger child had been weaned would she be allowed to visit the little grave in the cemetery at Jämaja.

Her unrest grew. Only once had she waited in such agony—for her sweetheart who had fled from conscription to a great, foreign vessel. Then she had run to and fro on the sands of Sõrve, in an agony of shame, alone, abandoned, watching the vessel recede into the horizon.

Tiiu opened hurriedly the door.

" Ingel, take thy heir."

She snatched the bundle from the girl's arms, danced it along the room, crushed it to her breast. For the first few moments it was enough for her to know that the child lived and that she could hold its tiny form in her lap.

But immediately afterwards, doubt and instinctive dread of the alien hands that had nursed the child awoke in her, and with it a desire to criticize, an impulse to find fault.

The light weight of the child astounded her, she could lift it easily over her head, it seemed to be without weight in her hands. She swung it to and fro as though appraising its weight.

How light it had become—hardly twenty pounds. . . .

Like a bundle of feathers. . . .

She began an agonized search for shortcomings, complaining, almost weeping at the same time. She undid the garments that wrapped it round, examining and criticizing each in turn.

" Poor boy, haven't they even patched his shirt—quite in rags."

" Hasn't seen water for a week . . ."

She stripped the child naked, examining its limbs.

It was bruised—there near the armpit—and there at the back of its knee.

"Good God, have they beaten the child—or let it fall and hurt itself?"

"The poor boy's arms are so thin too. Have they starved thee? Thy mother shall feed thee."

She sank on to a stool to suckle the child. While opening her robe she trembled with fear lest the child should refuse its nourishment.

The child looked at her wonderingly and gravely. It was used to lying alone, gazing at the ceiling, used to crying with no answer to its plaints; it was new to it to feel some one talking and fussing with it. It failed to understand what the occasion demanded. Restlessly its head moved to and fro, the tiny hands and feet stretched forth to ward off the stranger. Finally, its mouth twisted awry.

"Doesn't it want anything. Good Lord, does the child refuse me?"

It was as though she had lost her child, as though a second time it was torn from her. The child did not know her, feared her, she was without a child.

"Shall I take off the clasp—perhaps sonny

is afraid of it. Put on an old shawl—there, now does sonny know his own mother?"

"Does it want to ride, so : Sõit, sõit, Sõrve randa . . . kapp, kapp, kalaranda. . . ."

Steadily the boy refused all blandishments.

Nothing she did could bring a smile to the child's face.

Grave, prematurely aged, the child lay in her lap, as though the burden of its race already lay heavily upon it.

"Sonny grows up to be a man, becomes a fisherman at Sõrve. Brings silvery fishes from the sea. Mother cleans the fish and lays them in the sun to dry."

This too failed to attract the child. Ingel wept and sobbed in despair. All at once, a new thought awoke in her—a little, innocent thought.

"Mother will dress her son in fine garments, a gown of lace with blue bands."

The thought tickled her so that she rubbed her hands in glee. She began to search the drawers in which the little baron's clothes were kept, casting a medley of tiny garments on the floor—silken woolly, knitted, lace, tiny socks, coverlets, swaddling bands. She began to dress the child in them, seeking constantly anew, nothing seeming fine enough for her child. The whole drawer she turned upside down, searching for what she desired. A robe of gold it ought to have, like a king's child.

She was as happy as a maiden bedecking herself before a mirror. It was a delightful game, like dressing a big doll for a plaything.

At last the child was dressed, a gaudy rascal, dancing in her arms. No one would take him for a serf girl's child, a poor outcast, so like the baron's child he was. She placed the children side by side in the cradle and compared them. No difference whatever ; anyone might be mistaken, so gallant was the appearance of both.

She curtsied deeply, kissing her child's hand : Good morning, Gracious Baron. . . .

What should she do now, strip the child again ? Its former rags lay spread out on the bed ; an almost physical aversion made her shudder to look at them ; to touch them even with the finger-tip seemed unbearable. An unpleasant odour pervaded them.

A thought entirely new to her awoke. Why should one child lie clad in rags and another in silk ?

Her brain reeled as the thought developed. Never before had such ideas entered her mind. Who would dare to weigh God's works ? Still,

it was strange that the other child should remain
in this soft cradle and later trip through large,
light halls in fine footwear, and always have
sufficient food, though only goose-liver and honey
were good enough for it.   But the other, her own,
would return to the blackened, chimneyless hut,
play for a year or two on the shore of Sõrve,
pursuing sticklebacks in the shallows, and then
—slavery.

First as shepherd-boy on the herding-grounds,
following the manor cows, wetted by the rain
and shivering in the autumn.   Then as labour-
boy on the manor, still tender in frame and only
half-grown—doing a man's work, following the
plough, wielding a scythe.   Afterwards, he would
be given a hut and a patch of land, but not for
his own ; he would pay a rack-rent to the manor,
and when the lord should see fit he would be trans-
planted into the wilds to work for others again
as a colonist farmer.

She stood staring at the two children with
startled eyes.   Motherhood awakened a power
of prophecy within her, she became a seer, saw
visions of the future.   Her heart was nigh to
bursting at the thought of her son's fate.

Hate arose suddenly in her soul, although as
yet she knew not what she hated—bitterness,

desire for revenge.   She asked nothing for herself, willing to be trodden in the dust, but for her son she craved a better lot.

Then suddenly she snatched the little baron from his cradle and began to strip him of his finery with pitiless fingers, in feverish haste. Sky-blue robes, a down-edged smock were flung aside. The child cried in her grasp, unused to such hard treatment.

She wrapped her own child's rags around it— garments hardly holding together—a tattered shawl, a soiled shirt, a few old rags.   Her gentle, pliant nature suddenly turned fierce and pitiless.

She mocked and gloated over the child.

" Rag-doll—scarecrow !   Art thou now comfortable—sleep thou once in the rags of a labour-slave."

She enjoyed hugely the sight of the little baron's degradation ; it was as reparation, com-pensation for the whole of her race.   Coarse words welled over her lips, the very hearing of which would earlier have shocked her.

She raged at her fiercest, when Tiiu burst in sweating and pale with fear.

" All is lost—the Germans have unexpectedly come home, the mistress is already on the stair-case."

Ingel's brain became at once clear, as though she had been soused with cold water. All passion and heat vanished within the moment.

"Where shall we put the other child?" wailed Tiiu in distress. "And goodness knows . . ."

A cry broke from her at the sight of the little baron.

"Now thy back will be warmed, Ingel; not for anything would I be in thy skin."

Ingel had dropped on to the bed, deaf and blind to all around her. With eyes half-closed, beads of perspiration on her forehead, she seemed to be fighting out a battle within her.

"Hurry, the mistress is coming; I can hear steps in the corridor."

Ingel stood up. She had made her decision.

"Let the mistress come," she said slowly and with calm. "The mistress will beat me and drive me on the highway. Let her whip me and drive me away. I shall take my child and go."

The Death-Bed of Kubja-Pärt

KUBJA-PÄRT, THE BAILIFF OF Vaida, lay in his death agony.

In his own bed he lay, on a bundle of straw, beneath the sheepskins. No disease either, but only the common cold had laid him there. Coming from the tavern in a snowstorm he had strayed with his horse from the road into deep snowdrifts, and as it fought its way through these, his horse had slipped from between his knees and left him sitting on a ridge of snow as on a saddle. He was found the next day stiff as an icicle. And now his frozen limbs had thawed and he lay in his death agony.

Not many bailiffs could boast of dying in their own beds. Often they were found lying somewhere or other with bloody head—in deep hazelnut thickets or in the middle of a bog, or beaten to a jelly behind a barn. Their assailants were never known, the villagers holding their tongue as one man, all asserting their innocence at the inquiry. Arrest anyone if you can.

At times the hate towards a particular bailiff could grow until even assassination could not appease it—it had to break out as a malignant growth for all to see. In the bright light of day

94

he was attacked by a number of men together, in the fields at haymaking, or at the reaping, beaten to death, struck down, kicked even after life had left him, and then in a body all went to confess the deed. Not even three consecutive Sundays in the stocks or lifelong banishment to the land of ice—Siberia—could always hold back the people from open revenge.

Kubja-Pärt, however, had avoided every snare. Beneath his right armpit he might still feel on autumn nights sudden twinges in the scar left by a knife. On the approach of bad weather it glowed red and began to ache. Often he had engaged in hand-to-hand tussles on pitch-black nights, when it was impossible to see the assailant ; he could only feel his arms and the weight of his body.

Waiting for death, Kubja-Pärt thought of all these matters to pass the time, but the joy he experienced from them was less keen than in former days. Everything seemed vain now that he had fallen into the last snare of all, though one not laid by the labour-slaves.

Lying in his bed he gazed with weary eyes at Madli, his wife. They had no children. Had Madli once shaken his pillows or moved him in the bed ? Water, too, she fetched in a handleless cup, lukewarm insipid water of no use against thirst. Were he alone in the room, that black and sooty stone at the corner of the range would be as helpful to him as Madli.

"Madli, listen," he said ; " shalt thou be glad when I die ? "

" Not I ; but others will be glad—on the earth and beneath it."

" Dost thou mean that I shall go straight to Hell ? "

" Yes, and riding on a whip, of that thou canst be sure."

Kubja-Pärt opened wide his eyes. This was new to him. Madli had thus two reasons for pleasure : the first, that she would be free, the second, the certain knowledge of his destination.

" Why dost thou hate me ? Thou shouldst be thankful to me for saving thy honour, dregs of the gentry."

" The lord paid thee for me, as thou thyself knowest," his wife answered between her teeth.

" And what if I now repented all my evil deeds ? "

" Only that it would be a pity for the fire awaiting thee to be wasted."

" Madli, go and break off a rod or two—real

96

good rods—and bring them to me, my heart itches so strangely."

" It is thy hand that itcheth, but I am beyond thy reach ; try if thou canst touch me from the bed."

" Hear me, bring me rods."

" Dost thou need them for thyself ? In that case, I am a willing enough helper."

" Don't murmur, woman, do as I say. From the copse of young birches behind the mill. And tie them in readiness, remember."

" Why shouldn't I bring them ? The birches will have plenty of time to grow in peace after thy death."

A little later she returned with the rods, long, pliant, crackling birch-rods, such as were used at Vaida on whipping-days—Wednesdays and Saturdays.

Kubja-Pärt set them beside him in the bed.

" Look carefully now, Madli," he said. " Here are all my sins. I place them on my breast, see. And now thou believest I shall fly direct to Hell, with the rods on my chest, Madli."

He began fingering the rods and speaking of them to Madli.

" Many judgments have been carried out with these old friends. Backs have been beaten that were scarred by many earlier whippings, the scars opening as one struck. A man like that would often say not a word, take off his clothes himself, and cast himself on the bench in the stable—get on! It was like writing in blood on a back like that : no other documents needed, the skin as paper, the rod as a pen, and blood for ink, ready.

"But there were others, white as birch-bark, that trembled before the first stroke had alighted on them—little delicate maidens who wailed and moaned and embraced my knees. Often the clothes had to be torn in shreds from them, from neck to knee.

"All kinds of backs have been whipped with them, such as bore no sign of the whip. And when the rod strikes for the first time on such, a man can leap into the air like a two-year-old stallion that tastes the whip for the first time. But with time his spirit yields, and at the next stroke he clenches his teeth and does not budge."

"What if thou shouldst take them off again, Madli—they are beginning to be heavy," he said suddenly, turning his head on the pillow.

"Let them be—it is well that they weigh on thee also."

Man and wife gazed for a moment at each

other, the man's mouth twisting into a grin. His wife's certainty as to his damnation began to amuse him.

Suddenly, before the woman had time to prevent it, he managed to snatch the burning taper from the wall above him and set alight the rods on his chest with it.

They were slow to light ; the smaller twigs, burning and turning to charcoal, cast forth a thick black smoke, refusing to burst into open flame.

Kubja-Pärt swallowed the bitter smoke.

" See, Madli," he said, " here burn my sins, I place them over my heart. The smoke from them rises to Heaven, a sacrifice pleasant in the sight of the Lord."

He began to recite the Lord's Prayer in a voice half-suffocated.

" Thou thought'st I was surely damned, but I am on the way to Heaven," he whispered with malignant joy.

A moment later, Kubja-Pärt was dead. The rods still burned on his breast, crackling and shooting out little sparks.

The Trip to Town

NURGA MIHKEL SLOWLY DROVE A load of firewood from the manor to town. At times he sat on high upon his load, letting his feet dangle ; at times he walked beside it. He walked badly, his legs bending at the knees and giving at each step. In appearance, he was long and slender, with shoulders slightly bowed, and hanging lower lip.

Man, horse and load were hidden by a thick covering of dust : the road was like a flour-bin, clouds of dust arising at each step. Large and angry gad-flies swarmed round the horse on all sides, and settled on its thin flanks and bony limbs. Mihkel let drive at them now and then with a birch-branch and swore at intervals, even, at times, forcing the horse into a loose canter to escape them.

On both sides the land was dry pasturage, a drought of many weeks having passed over it as a raging fire. The bare soil gaped in places as though charred. For a couple of versts the road ran between the manor fields, already in stubble, the shocks of rye beginning to dry in the faint wind.

Mihkel looked long at the shocks with mingled

envy and indifference. The other day he had himself been employed in reaping the manor fields. Yesterday he had been able to commence a corner of his own field, to reap a couple of plots, and now this trip to town had interrupted his work.

A peculiar feeling clutched his heart each time he thought of his own fields. Small narrow strips of land around patches of quagmire, badly drained, badly ploughed. Even the grain differed from the manor grain, growing as it did sparse and short in the stalk and with empty ears. And yet this year the seed had been good and there had been enough of it, for the sprouts had shown as a thick green carpet. But then had come a dry summer. A burning sun had blazed for ever in a cloudless sky, the mornings had been thick with sun-dust, and the whole atmosphere had seemed to boil and vaporize. The rye had ripened half-grown, the half-soft grain shedding from the ear. Next year's bread had dropped slowly to the ground.

They had called on the gracious master, first singly, then as a deputation, hats in hand already on the highway : " Gracious Baron-lord, the rye drops from the ears." His Grace gazes sternly at them, waves his hand : " For this same reason every man shall reap the manor fields to-morrow—every man." They crept out by the door, with heads hanging like those of old work-horses, and in each mind rose the image of the small ſtrips of land around the bogs. But the following day they reaped in the sweat of their brows the rye on the manor fields.

Nurga Mihkel reached the church at Kaarma, whence it was ſtill twelve verſts to the town of Kuresaare. The horse ſtopped unbidden and laid back its ears with its shaggy mane turned towards the left. From behind a low building of ſtone came the whinny of another horse. Nurga Mihkel's horse whickered in reply, and began to drag itself towards the sound.

" All right then, as the gelding wishes it too."

Nurga Mihkel turned his horse towards the tavern, which rose darkly, punĉtuated by small windows, in the shadow of the church. For many decades they had ſtared at one another, the tavern and the church—the church upright, noble, crushing, the tavern grovelling and hiding its wrath.

After tying up his horse, Mihkel went ſtraight into the tavern-room, with his slow and shaky tread. The room was cool and dark as a cellar, the ſtone walls breathed chilliness, the floor was formed of broad uneven slabs of ſtone.

"Vodka," said Mihkel heavily, sitting down on a bench.

From the opposite corner a man arose, in coachman's attire, a coat with shiny buttons and a high hat.

"Good-day, Nurga Mihkel, whither away?"

"To town. . . ."

The man took off his hat, releasing his curly hair. His face was broad and ruddy, his cheeks bright-red, with a second chin beginning to sag beneath the first. His eyes were small, lustful and shifty. He fixed them on Mihkel half in scrutiny, half in mockery, as though to measure the peasant's stupidity. He swung his feet, cast one across another, and began to hum. It was as though a thought was developing in his mind, awakened by the sight of Mihkel.

"On thine own business?" he continued his examination.

"No—the manor wood. . . ."

Mihkel was quite unaware of the other's glances as he slowly drank his vodka in small economical gulps.

"Why dost thou shake thy head so, man?"

"The grain is dropping," Mihkel answered monotonously, as though repeating ancient history with no thought of seeking sympathy or of

103

being understood. At the same time he glanced for the first time at the coachman sitting opposite. An instinctive repulsion awoke in him. A parasite this of the gentry. A man who ate pure bread throughout the year.

" Thou shouldst have reaped it earlier—made makeshift bread of it."

The coachman uttered this lightly, indifferently, baring his white teeth at the thought of bread that burns like straw when ignited.

Then he bent suddenly forward, close to Mihkel's face.

" Listen, Mihkel, dost want to earn fifteen kopeks ? "

Mihkel withdrew a little, as far as the wall allowed. He delayed answering, weighing the matter, as one struggling against suspicion that knocked faintly at his mind.

" Only—for taking this letter to the judge."

The coachman drew forth a letter with five seals from his breast pocket.

" I should not have time to go now—that's why, thou seest—and thou art going to town in any case—a letter doesn't weigh anything," he continued.

He moved round Mihkel, as a man might round a girl whose interest he wished to gain.

His eyes gleamed small and enticing beneath his heavy brows. Thus doubtless he looked at girls when he would win their favour. The Lovelace in him was uppermost at the moment, the resistless will that none could withstand or fetter.

"Give it here—happen I shall have time to take it."

Mihkel stretched out in all innocence his hand for the letter and the money. For a moment he still suspected mischief : why should the other be so insistent ?—he would have taken the letter with less persuading. But the tiny round silver coin hastened his decision, a peculiar feeling of pleasure flowed through his being as the coin slid into his hand, slightly cold, like a drop of water to the palm. It was nearly new, shiny and glittering even in the shadows.

"A pleasant journey," the coachman called after him.

Mihkel sat crossways on his load again. Why should the coachman laugh so ? See, there he was roaring with mirth now at the door so that his whole body writhed. And why should he shout so often : "A pleasant journey" ?

Then his misgivings against the coachman awoke in him again. "What a rascal, advising a man to bake makeshift bread, as though he had

not eaten enough of it when he was no higher
than that." But it was so, after a few years at
the Germans' table, bread was no longer good
enough, nor salted fish. The peasant, anxious
over his fields, was laughed at.

Mihkel's gorge rose at the coachman's indifference, at his complete unconcern over the seasons
and weather, over droughts and frosts. His
peasant instincts were offended at such airs of
gentility, and his own inward dread with which
he watched the changes of heat and cold and wind
and cloud gnawed at his heart more bitterly.
Vagrant . . .

Yet, in spite of all, a slight sensation of pleasure
began to arise in him. Was it the vodka that
coursed so pleasantly in his veins, or the knowledge of the little silver coin in his coat pocket?
What could he not buy with the money? . . .
First, flounders for five kopeks, the fish accursed
of the Saviour, which melted so well, however,
in the mouth of an islander. For such an outlay
he would obtain many; the wife would even be
able to salt part of them, to lay them in the tub
in layers like brown leaves.

Tobacco he would also buy and vodka again
on his homeward way. He would enter the
tavern, throw down a coin on the table, and say:

"Vodka for two kopeks, cost what it may." If the Vaida coachman had been there, he would have shared with him also. . . .

The nearer he drew to the town, the more did a light intoxication steal over him, for his body, weary with constant labour and thin with lifelong starvation, lacked all power to struggle against it ; a glass of anything stronger than water was enough to make such as he merry.

Driving up the narrow street he even tried to sing, he felt himself drawn towards all the world, as he stared maudlin at the passers-by. Then all at once he began to regard the duty imposed on him by the coachman as a matter of honour, a trust given lightly to no man. To be sure the man had heard how trustworthy Nurga Mihkel was, no thief, no liar, no coveter of other's possessions. . . . Some one had doubtless said : "Look at Nurga Mihkel, that is a man. . . . Another might lose the letter, let it fall on the highway, might take it from his pocket—so— and before you could explain, it would have slipped on to the highway—be left there—for some old gipsy woman or such-like to find."

Any other would certainly open it, if it came to that. His own fingers itched as he gazed at it ; he longed to see the writing, even though he understood nothing but that it was black on white. But those five red patches, they would break on opening. They said a man could be sent to prison for such an act. The Baron of Vaida had set them there with his own fingers ; he could see the Vaida crest on them, the same as was carved in limestone on the gable of the Vaida manor, a bear carrying a crown.

He would refuse to give the letter to a servant, but would demand to see the judge himself. He would even wipe his hand on his coat tails before taking out the letter, and then holding it genteelly from a corner between two finger-tips, he would blow the dust from it.

" Most Gracious Judge-Lord, here is the Vaida Baron's letter."

He would bow deeply, almost to the ground. Perhaps the judge would tip him, who knows, dig up from his pocket a couple of copper coins, or even a half, and place it in his hand saying : " Here, drink my health at the Kaarma tavern."

Mihkel shook with inward laughter at the fancy. He began to withdraw all he had thought regarding the Vaida coachman ; the man was an honest and a fine fellow, although he was too eager after the girls and was a babbler. What could he be expected to know of a peasant's cares, a man who fed his horses from morning to night, groomed and washed them, and at times drove round the parish to show off the buttons of his coat that gleamed and glittered. What could a man like that know. But he took thought for a poor devil—presented him with fifteen kopeks . . .

Having taken his load of wood to its destination, he made a simple toilet in the yard of a posting-house, gleaning the straws and wisps of hay from his garments. Holding his head high, he inquired of all he met where the judge lived, in a voice loud enough to be heard over the street, and with the letter in his hand that all might see the seals.

His spirit remained undaunted up to the judge's stairway, but then at each step it began to fail. At each step the judge seemed to him to become higher and mightier and he himself to shrink. He no longer dared to think of the door up to which the steps were leading him. He turned dizzy, and his knees knocked together as though he were climbing upwards to the clouds. He seemed already to see the judge sitting as on the arch of the sky with the scales of justice in his hand and thundering forth his judgments.

Almost before he knew, he was in the hall and

a servant had snatched the letter from him. He grasped what had happened only when it was too late. Yet once aware of it, it seemed almost a relief. He had turned already towards the door, and was fumbling with the catch in order to slink out when heavy footsteps and a jingle of spurs made him stop.

"Here, you fellow—you are to have forty brace of stripes," some one said in a loud voice.

Nurga Mihkel's mouth opened, and he stood as though fallen from the clouds, unable to say a word.

"It is written here : driven a three-year gelding to ruin ; forty brace of stripes at the judge's in town."

Nurga Mihkel was still unable to understand. Three-year geldings driven furiously by him, his own old horse lumbering after them ! What did it all mean ? He stared helplessly at the judge, a short bald-headed man in uniform.

"Who is to be whipped ? " he stammered.

"You—seize him, men."

Two soldiers sprang at him from either side. His intoxication left him instantly, he became fully sober.

"Gracious Judge-Lord, I am innocent ; I am not the man," he shouted, trying desperately to free himself.

" What does he say ? " asked the judge, who had already turned to go.

" Let me go, I am innocent—the Vaida coachman . . ."

The Judge hesitated a moment and then shrugged his shoulders.

" Innocent or guilty—how am I to know ? I have my duty to perform."

He waved to the men—they began to drag the struggling Mihkel away, resisting with arms and legs, still protesting his innocence. They cast him on a hard bench, strapped him down, tore open his garments and the blows began to fall. He felt as though fire rained on him—as though he lay naked in a thunderstorm and the lightning struck down on him. Before his eyes stars danced on a background of blackest night. Something warm trickled down his ribs and dripped upon the floor. Blood. . . . Then time had become as Eternity—doubtless he had already received hundreds of strokes. . . . Perhaps the men had become mixed in their account and would beat him to death, as they did the Vaida thresher. . . . He would have wept from fury and pain. . . . A strange weakness stole through his limbs, his feet and hands and head were as if lost and forgotten. . . . His head was numb, as though not a drop of blood remained there. . . .

" Forty," soughed in his ears.

He lay without stirring and struggled to his feet only after a soldier had thrust at his ribs.

Dully, without a murmur, he threw on his clothes and turned to go.

" Ahoy, fellow—fifteen kopeks for the rods," some one shouted after him.

He looked round stupidly and then began to understand. The whole of his wrongs stood clear before him. But whom to blame for his misfortunes, he himself could not have said. The Vaida coachman who had deceived him, the gentleman who had had him whipped unheard, or the soldiers who had carried out the sentence.

At the same time he was ashamed, his own stupidity vexed him most. And should the story of it be spread about, the people would laugh at him to his face, laugh and admire the coachman for his trick—a bright fellow, see how well he could deceive another man and save his own skin. . . . What would not a labour-slave pay for a good laugh ? . . . No one would blame the gentry ; who could hope to reach them, working as they did above the clouds, like God the

Father Himself ? . . . Better to be silent as the grave. . . .

He fished up the silver coin slowly, breathed on it, polished it with the sleeve of his coat. It was hard to part with it ; almost would he have suffered the whole punishment over again to be allowed to keep the fifteen kopeks.

At last he sighed deeply, turned away, and slid the coin into a soldier's hand.

Half an hour later he drove his empty cart at a half-trot along the road to Kaarma.

What thoughts were his ? He could not think. At the most the platform of his bath-hut shone like a mirage in his mind, its steaming, heated, moist atmosphere and the hiss of the water thrown by his wife on the glowing stones. And he himself stretched out on his stomach, his wife rubbing his back with vodka and beating out the perspiration with a scented bundle of birch twigs.

"Was it our own lord that had thee whipped ? " his wife would ask.

Whereat he would reply : "Our own or others—what does it matter ? Look thou to the heat, hag."

The Parish Clerk and the Vicar

THE VICAR OF KAARMA, VON ROSEN, sat in his study noting recent deaths in the church register. He felt hot, despite the cool cellar-like atmosphere of his study and the open window whose curtains not a breath of air stirred. The room was narrow, badly lighted, and a scent of damp earth and rock lingered in its corners. The light played in green reflections on the white-washed walls, after traversing the bushes which clustered round the window. The study was a gloomy place, like the whole vicarage, built as it was within the walls of a nunnery that had stood since Roman Catholic times. The vaulted hall with its rounded arches remained to remind men of the former convent.

Von Rosen turned over the pages of the Register with an ill grace and absently : Anna Ei-tea, forty years ; Riidu, the son of Mihkel, two years three months. . . . Half-audibly he translated the Parish Clerk's answers from Estonian into German, taking no heed of him, as at each muttered remark he unconsciously turned his left ear to the speaker, that being his best ear. The Vicar knew that the Parish Clerk understood and could even speak German to some extent, but to keep up the deep chasm between them he invariably spoke in the Estonian language.

The Parish Clerk stood in the centre of the room answering an occasional question of the Vicar's, a small roll of paper in his hand—a withered man of short stature, dressed in homespun, with an air at once humble and intelligent. He stood without support, evidently tired as from time to time he shifted his weight from one foot to the other.

Von Rosen never glanced at him, but marked down the names of dead in a special list and drew crosses accompanied by the date of death in the book. Everything was done with the greatest possible slowness and with dignity. He sat in a comfortable chair upholstered in leather and let his feet sprawl loosely on the floor. As a matter of fact, he worked mechanically, his thoughts being taken up by an even humming that proceeded from somewhere behind the building. This humming, with which there mingled an incessant chirruping from a neighbouring bush, excited him, keeping his senses strung. It burbled like a boiling kettle, hissing monotonously, uninterruptedly, with a slight hint of a whine in its note. He listened to each shade of its music, awaiting a change in its register.

The day was as though chosen for the purpose—cloudless, hot, with no breath of a wind under the sky . . . rain was not to be feared. It was inevitable that the bees should swarm that day, those at leaſt in the raspberry bushes, where the great family kept house. If all went well, he would double his swarms this summer. The winter had proved too severe for many, much too long, so that the bees had ſtarved. He added up in his head how many pounds of honey he would obtain from each hive. Perhaps there would be sufficient to warrant a personal journey to Riga to dispose of it.

He caſt a sidelong glance at the Parish Clerk, and the keen, though ſtill humble, gaze that he met irritated him. Did the man guess his thoughts? He became doubly grave and, as though he were alone in the room, repeated the Parish Clerk's words in a loud voice. His ruddy features, like those of the saints in the cheap gaudy oleographs that hung in the homes of the people, became grave and ſtern.

The little withered Parish Clerk had often before caused him discomfort. There was nothing in the man on which he could pounce, the whole of him seeming in some wise only skin and bone, not to be gripped anywhere. Owing to his deficient knowledge of Estonian, von Rosen, when he made his pastoral rounds, was extremely dependent on him, and he could never forgive him the mortification which had once befallen him at a funeral.

They had stood together with the mourners round the funeral feast, with grave expressions fitted to the occasion, long rows of serious stern visages. He had himself begun the Lord's Prayer as a blessing, reciting from memory. And then suddenly had felt his memory fail him, the words he sought to utter became entangled, like threads in a hopeless knot ; he stammered, perspired, and felt the veins stand out on his forehead. . . . He had repeated the last sentence—unavailingly. He had gazed helplessly round the room, each face seeming like a judge to accuse him. And at last his glance had rested on the Parish Clerk at the other end of the table :

" Johanson, continue for me," he had found strength to say.

Instead of gratitude for the assistance he had then received, in his anger he had selected the Parish Clerk as a victim, laying the blame for his own disgrace wholly on the latter's shoulders. He had been humbled before his parishioners, and the matter had been widely discussed in the parish, spread doubtless by his Parish Clerk.

Further, it seemed to him at times as though the Clerk viewed his many secular activities with disapproval, though naturally without open comment. The man had peculiarly keen eyes in his withered face, flashing penetrating eyes that followed the Vicar at suitable and unsuitable seasons.

Certainly, he was a farmer before all, despite his priestly office ; that much was plain. In the face of usual custom he had kept the vicarage lands for himself instead of letting them out as the majority of his predecessors had done. He was of an impoverished noble family which had gradually been evicted from its estates, and his choice of a priestly career had been dictated chiefly by ambition to live as a landowner notwithstanding. He was interested in farming, knowing its many phases and never hesitating to take part in the work himself.

He was doubly feared by his workpeople. In the first place he always took part in the work and nothing escaped his glance, so that with him no subterfuge could avail. There were two whipping-days at the manse as at the manors. They invented a saying for him :

"Let us chasten the body to-day—the soul to-morrow."

But they were used to harsh masters, and alone, this fact would not have been sufficient to scare them. They were afraid yet more of his sermons, and of the terrors of Hell with which he threatened those who disobeyed their masters. They believed him to hold the keys of Heaven, opening its gates for those he willed to enter. One subject alone provided the material for his most burning and convincing sermons : the indolence and ingratitude of the peasants. At such times his beautiful deep voice resounded through the church, causing the women in the left-hand benches to weep. If the matter had depended on him, he would have kept in force an old decree of Catherine II, which forced the people to attend a service of repentance at the churches twice a year, the subject-matter for the sermon, laid down in the law, being the obedience due from slaves to their gentle-born owners. He would hardly have needed, however, to do this, the old method of compulsion having obtained such a hold on the people that even after its abolition they continued to fill the church on the approved dates.

And yet von Rosen was not hated quite as

much as might have been expected, the peasants feeling a kind of liking for him despite their fear. His expert knowledge in every branch of agriculture was not without its effect on them, and also, he was not afraid himself of the roughest labour. But above all they were influenced by his outward appearance, their spirits rising at the sight of his face which, despite the scolding mouth, bore the stamp of an unspeakable satisfaction with life and himself, a gleam of something resembling kindheartedness shining in his large gentle eyes.

The only person whom he had found it impossible to frighten and incidentally to vanquish was this little Parish Clerk. In him he divined a secret resistance and defiance : he was neither peasant nor gentleman. The very fact that he was neither annoyed von Rosen. He could not see his way to scold him to his face as he did the peasants, but still less could he demean himself to treat him as an equal. True, he made him stand in his presence, and emphasized the familiar " thou " to keep the Clerk aware of his lowly station, but even then it seemed as though the man was not sufficiently humbled.

Their fiercest battles were concerned with the peasants. The Clerk never defended them

openly, but never failed to bring to his superior
new charges and complaints, as though he purposely scoured the village for these. He made
them meekly, without noise, as though it were
the moſt natural thing on earth to discuss such
matters with his spiritual father. Now it was
a four-day labourer who had been evicted from
his plot, now a girl whom the maſter of Vaida
had compelled to yield him his rights.

"What has it to do with thee?" the Vicar
had once burſt out.

"With me, nothing, but with you, Your
Grace," the Clerk had replied.

Von Rosen was so used to the grovelling and
dog-like submission of the lower orders, that a
silent resiſtance of this description was new to
him. He loved to see the peasants, at the mere
sound of the bells on the manse carriage shafts
—such bells were forbidden the peasants—drive
ſtraight into the ditches edging the highway so
that their cartloads scattered in all directions.
He loved to see them approach him with bowed
backs and remove their headwear at the manse
gate, embracing his knees with both hands in
thankfulness.

A secret oppression often possessed him when
alone with his Clerk, though he was careful to

show nothing of this. The man was tough, strong, with a kind of elasticity that lifted him from his lowly station ; he could never be crushed to the earth ; he knew how to be silent and abide his time.

Who could say but that by just such men and their descendants the power of the Germans would some day be broken in the country? They were the moles attacking in all silence the foundations.

Hardly had this one risen half a step in the social scale before he stood firmly there and seemingly intended to lift the rest of the multitude as high.

A sweltering heat streamed through the window, the whitewashed stone walls became hot as the walls of an oven. The Parish Clerk shifted his weight oftener from foot to foot ; he had stood at least for half an hour and the heat pressed at his temples like a band of iron. As though by accident and stealthily he glanced at an empty chair at the table's corner, but quickly turned his eyes. No thought of sitting down had been in his mind, and yet the chair drew his gaze so that he had to struggle against looking as against a temptation. His eyes took in the room stealthily, and fell on the great cupboard where the registers and appliances for Holy Communion were preserved. Slowly his arm moved, his elbow feeling for the edge of the cupboard, leaning at first cautiously and lightly, then with gathering strength until at last it so lay on a ledge that it supported a good part of his weight.

Von Rosen looked up suddenly.

"Johanson—what art thou thinking of? Stand up straight, canst thou not see I am present?"

He was delighted at the splendid opportunity to humble the Clerk and to crush him completely, the chance he had long awaited.

The Clerk withdrew his arm calmly from the cupboard's edge and stood upright, arms hanging, without a tremor in his face.

At the same time a hissing murmur was heard from the garden, as though a stone had been cast in a seething cauldron and caused the water to boil over.

Von Rosen was on his feet within a second. Tearing off his coat he rushed into the garden, leaving the Clerk standing in the centre of the study floor.

"The bees, the bees!" his echoing shout sounded from the garden.

The garden of the Kaarma manse was in direct contrast to its fields, as uncared for and wild as they were cultivated. Von Rosen cared little for it ; everything grew at its will, even the weeds. In the rich soil nettles flourished, so rank that they hid the wall, as tall as strange and rare plants trained by careful culture. The strawberries had, on their part, run wild in their freedom, and escaping from their beds had trailed at random over the edges of the paths with long, limp tendrils that bore no fruit.

In the shadow of the high raspberry bushes thick with unripe fruit, a dozen or so beehives had been erected, pieces of the hollowed trunks of trees, from which a mysterious murmur now proceeded. These old-fashioned hives retained something of the scented poesy of the forests, bringing to mind a primeval wood where all is life, even to the rotting stumps of trees.

Above the raspberry bushes a little dark cloud floated, expanding and contracting, hissing and humming, like the sound of hundreds of needles being ground together. Seen closer, it resembled a black net with meshes in constant motion, to and fro ; swarming bees at play.

Suddenly the whole swarm darted forward, swift as an arrow.

" They are flying over the fence—the mirror, quickly," thundered von Rosen.

He had forgotten everything, the dark study with its scent of mildew, dusty registers and mutinous Parish Clerk. All trace of clerical leisure left his limbs, as despite a growing tendency to stoutness he sprang backwards and forwards, panting and blowing. He had already succeeded in snatching a syringe, and climbing the low stone wall he directed its nozzle towards the fleeing swarm.

A thin drizzle of water fell over the bees ; they seemed to hesitate, floating for a while in one spot, seemed to be holding a council.

Von Rosen tore the mirror from the hand of a servant and began to twirl it in the sun, the sunbeams ricochetting from its shining surface and falling straight on the bees in sudden flashes, quick as lightning.

A memory of the Parish Clerk assailed von Rosen for the space of a moment. What nonsense, naturally the man had gone, he comforted himself. Or had busied himself with some occupation there. What annoyed him was that he had again given the man cause for comment.

The entire swarm was now streaming round a luxuriant lime. Suddenly, they encircled a jutting limb and began to wrap themselves around it, clinging fast to one another, seeming to form a plant in movement, a brown lichen suddenly sprouting from the branch. The lichen spread till, finally, a large quivering growth, increasing each moment in size, hung down along the tree trunk.

Von Rosen remained at least an hour in the garden, from which no earthly power could have drawn him. The swarming of bees was a passion with him, exciting him as if it had been a well-organized pastime. Not until everything was in order, the new family comfortably in its dwelling, could he prevail on himself to return to the study for his coat.

In the centre of the study floor stood the Parish Clerk, in the position in which the Vicar had left him.

Von Rosen stood speechless with amazement, he had again forgotten the clerk's existence.

" What art thou doing here ? " he finally burst out.

" Standing and waiting, Your Grace," the Parish Clerk replied.

Von Rosen fell gasping into his chair and stared at the Clerk. Was the man mocking him ? He could not make out whether biting irony or the greatest meekness had dictated his words. And why had he stood the whole time ?

To show his bodily endurance, or from fear, from the workings of a submissive slave soul?

Or was there something hidden? Was the clerk truly a man with the patience to bide his time, to stand and wait? And behind him long rows of silent men, clad in homespun. . . . And when the time had come—what then?

The Sacrifice

IT ALL HAPPENED IN A REMOTE
fishing-village, far from the manor, far from
the church, still more distant from the only town
on the island, on a sand-flat where the only occasional visitor, rare at that, was a strayed grey seal,
escaped from the seal-hunting Swedes of Ruhnu.

A rumour began to circulate at haymaking
time, that Sooru Andres was afflicted with the
leprosy.

Sooru Andres, a fisherman, whose chimneyless hut was nearest the net-drying grounds, had
suffered for many years from occasional fits of
languor, that grew latterly to pains radiating
through his whole body, while at the same time
flecks of brown, which vanished when pressed
with the finger, began to appear on his arms.
At first he paid no regard to these symptoms, and
took part in the fishing as before, having, beside
his wife, three children to keep, but at the end of
a year he had grown worse. An old hag, who
performed the duties of a quack doctor, was
called, and he was thoroughly sweated in the
bath-house, his children peeping through the
cracked panes to watch their father undergoing
massage. Andres himself said nothing, his large

powerful frame lying on the bath platform in the hands of the women-folk, as he submitted without a murmur at his treatment.

At that time, he was close on forty, and had lived till then healthy and strong.

For a little while his health improved and for a whole spring he worked at the fishing, but coming home early one summer morning from the nets, he got for himself a bowl filled with water, and frowning in the effort, began to examine his features as reflected in the bowl, rubbing the back of his hand across his eyebrows, the skin of which was swollen to a shiny purple, so that the hairs had totally disappeared.

Having looked his fill without uttering a word, he kicked over the bowl on the threshold and ordered Tiiu, his wife, shortly : " Take it away."

After this, he arranged a bed for himself before the fire, complaining of pangs of cold that never left him, and lying there he stared with eyes half-hidden by heavy drooping lids through the mist of smoke at those moving in the hut.

The brown patches on his arms had become little aching swellings, and like swellings began to show also in his face, transforming it beyond recognition.

The whole village came to see him, the women

oftener, the men more seldom. Some tried to scare him, others consoled him, while a third group gave good advice, all of which he followed, with a great and submissive patience, swallowing the many horrible and unpalatable medicines concocted for him.

After a time he was up and about again, working the whole winter at small household tasks, weaving baskets and mending nets, but in the following haymaking period he took to his bed again, complaining this time of fever. His face seemed, also, strangely shiny, as though swollen, the skin stretched tightly over his altered features ; swollen too were his hands and feet.

He understood then, and with him the whole village, that he suffered from leprosy, and throughout the village a feeling of helplessness and impending doom spread, as though at the approach of a great and merciless affliction for them all. And many examined their hearts in the light of the Scriptures, seeking for hidden sins, for which punishment now was nigh, a punishment that included the whole village. Mothers, fearstricken, bathed their children in the bath-house, searching their bodies from crown to toe, seeking for signs of the dread disease, alarmed at the slightest wound. No

one, on the other hand, dreamed of sending for a
doctor, the village being situated at the farthest
end of Sõrve, behind the sand-plains and wilds,
where each one lived and died as it were on his
own resources, without outside help.

Andres' wife Tiiu, with the latest child, hardly
a year old, on her arm, went from neighbour to
neighbour until she had visited every one in the
village. A thick fog enveloped the wide sand-
flat with its nets and osier fish-traps that evening, leaving visible only the wings of the three
windmills in the village floating on the surface
of mist, swimming in a ghostly sea of white.

Reinu Kaarel's big goat strayed from the flock
and catching its horns in an osier trap was held
there the whole night, until in the morning a
shepherd boy released the trembling animal,
which, half dead with fright, staggered about for
a while on the shore and then disappeared into
the forest.

And Teiste Mari was visited by a nightmare
in the shape of a fine horsehair sieve, from which
flour dripped, white as chalk, filling the eyes
and the nostrils, choking the breath and blinding
one.

The whole fishing village was awake that
night except the children, pondering the ways

of God and seeking a way out of the approaching affliction.

The following day was a Sunday, the fog departing and leaving the village in its setting of glittering white sand. None of the men prepared for church, but all the morning they sat on the drying-ground, surrounded by a dozen or so grey sheds for the nets, the empty net-poles stretching in lines in all directions, like rows of thin crosses.

They discoursed among themselves, a silent and gloomy council to which the women were not invited, weighed down by responsibility for the prosperity or destruction of the village entrusted to their care. Among them were many who had grown up from childhood with Andres and many of his near relatives, while almost all were of the same fishing set, with common fishing waters and common nets and traps.

At midday, when the women returned from church, they sent word for Andres to join them, pointing out a place for him outside of their own circle, on the threshold of a ramshackle shed.

No one showed any eagerness to begin, all being good comrades and the scourge seeming a common punishment for all, perhaps for the sins of all present, so that no one could be certain that the next time he or his house might not be singled out, for they knew villages in which there were five or six or even more lepers.

But when they saw the appealing and down-cast eyes of the sick man, longer silence became impossible and the eldeſt fisherman present spoke, the others putting away their pipes while he did so :

" We all know that thou art a leper."

Again all were silent and across the sky ſtartled fleeing clouds floated, juſt over their heads.

The eldeſt spoke again :

" We are altogether almoſt forty souls, count-ing children, and thou art one.   Is it not more fit that one be sacrificed than that a whole people be deſtroyed ?

" Look thou, our intention is not to deſtroy thee, but to provide thee with food and drink until thy death.   But that thou mayeſt not infeċt us all, likewise thy wife and children, we shall confine thee in Reinu Kaarel's old ſtable and we believe thee to be willing to submit peaceably to our will ? "

Then no one uttered a word, neither judges nor the bejudged, as in this council there were neither lawyers nor speeches in defence, and the wind drove the flying sand in a golden sunlit cloud into their eyes, and gulls flew searching for fish offal over the drying-ground, where men were engaged in giving word to God's judgment.

The following day was as fine as the day that went before, filled with the glitter of sea and sun. The children danced all morning from one hut to the other in the loose sand. Reinu Kaarel, at the other end of the village, dug out the refuse from his stable, replacing it with straw. The greater part of the fishers had remained at home but had kept indoors, appearing sometimes at the doors of their huts, and uneasily glancing towards the house of Reinu Kaarel. The women fetched water from each other's wells and whispered, their red-striped skirts bright in the sun.

At one o'clock, Reinu Kaarel accompanied by an old, white-bearded fisherman arrived at Sooru Andres' hut. Neither entered. Reinu Kaarel only pushed the door slightly ajar and called : " Come out."

The first to appear were the three elder children of Andres, two boys and a girl, who thrust their heads out of the door for a moment and then fled inside. A moment later all three came out singly and taking up a position near the driftwood pile waited grave and curious for what was to come.

Otherwise, not a movement in the hut. Reinu Kaarel sat down on the chopping block and lit his pipe, the white-bearded fisherman gazed at the sunlit sea with eyes half-closed.

Of a sudden Andres came out hurriedly, in his most worn garments, and with a small bundle under his arm. Then the youngest of the children began to cry and in a moment all three were weeping together.

"Tiiu, take the children," Andres commanded in the hoarse voice of the leper.

But the children had already hurried ahead, running along the lane to the other end of the village, still crying, a dozen scared sheep fleeing before them.

Andres set out between Reinu Kaarel and the white-bearded fisherman and slightly in front of them, Tiiu following behind, sobbing and carrying her baby.

As they passed the straw-thatched chimneyless huts, curious and grave faces appeared round corners. First one and then another joined the procession, straggling slightly behind, but a group of barelegged children trotted close to the leaders.

"Begone, children," shouted Reinu Kaarel.

The children drew back behind the stone foundation of a windmill and from there raced over the stone fence towards Reinu Kaarel's hut.

Andres said not a word, and none of his followers spoke. At the bend of the road, the white-bearded one stopped and offered Andres a match.

Suddenly, Andres' shaggy sheep-dog came, giving tongue loudly and, howling as though divining the evil to come, clung with both paws to its master's knees.

"Tie up the dog," Andres said. One of the rearguard, which had now grown to at least ten, seized the dog and shut it in an adjoining shed, where it began to howl and scratch at the door with its claws.

The procession turned towards the sandy heath, slow, gloomy as a funeral, sinking in the loose sand at each step. Others came in sight along the shore, a group of over ten without counting children.

Reinu Kaarel's hut stood on the farthest edge of the village, larger and better built than the others. An old, unused and dilapidated stable stood apart from the other buildings, in a treeless clearing with door thrown open.

A silence as of the grave prevailed, broken only by the distant howls of the imprisoned dog.

"Dost thou now go voluntarily and is it thine

own true will ? " the white-bearded fisherman asked.

" It is," came in answer from the leper.

Some of the women peeped in at the stable door, retreating quickly, but a couple of urchins slipped in, and were dragged out by Kaarel.

Then of a sudden, all eyes were drawn to Tiiu, who had sunk to the ground and now wept with shrill, nerve-shaking wailing, her baby rolling on the sand beside her.

" Quickly, quickly," Reinu Kaarel urged the old fishermen.

Each grasped Andres by a shoulder and began pushing him towards the open door of the stable. As though gathering all his strength, Andres shook them from him with one movement of his shoulders, stepping of his own accord through the doorway, without another glance behind him.

At that, Reinu Kaarel hurriedly took out a padlock which he had kept in his pocket till then and made as though to lock the door, when Andres suddenly turned.

" Wait, there is a boy here," he said.

And from the darkest corner of the stable, where he lay on a bundle of straw, he drew a boy of six, tousled and tearstained, his own boy who had hidden himself there.

He handed out the boy and Reinu Kaarel locked the door with the great padlock, placing the key in his pocket.

They all stood with bared heads as at a sacred ceremony, piously as their ancestors had stood centuries ago in their sacred groves, sacrificing to angry gods, and the voice of Teiste Mari was uplifted in a hymn sung only at funerals, and they sang through its seven verses from beginning to end, a slow, long-drawn dirge, before the locked stable.

The Smuggler

PARBU-JAAN, THE SMUGGLER, SAT on a bench in the cell for prisoners awaiting trial, expecting each moment to be called before the judge. His square-clipped sailor's beard rested every now and then on the thick shawl wrapped twice round his throat ; at each slightest movement his stiff oilskin coat crackled. Weary with waiting, he let his eyes wander over the wall of the cell, but soon desisted, finding that he knew the room as well as his own fisherman's hut on the shore of Kihelkonna ; it was the third time that he sat within these walls. He glanced for a moment at his companions—two youths playing cards at the other end of the room. In reality they were pretending to be occupied by the game, the while they watched him with grinning faces, and open, boyish curiosity in their eyes. Parbu-Jaan weighed them up a moment with keen eyes, accustomed to look far over vast stretches of sea, and to which all objects seemed too close, a frown drawing his brows together as though he weighed the two lads and found them wanting in the balance.

Quickly, however, his face, expressive of cunning and determination, became wreathed in smiles and filled with good humour. He rose and paced across the room a couple of times, saying as he passed the youths :

" Stealing wood from the manor forest, hey ? "

Tolerant forgiveness of the crime and contempt for its insignificance were mingled in his tone.

" Hit the nail right on the head," one of the youths said braggingly, and aping manliness.

Parbu-Jaan did not deign to look at them, but halted and stood tall beneath the barred window set high in the wall, his stalwart frame, over six feet high, seeming to fill the room, and cast a giant shadow over all in it. His height enabled him to reach the window and to rest his chin on the ledge of stone, and for a moment he stood there motionless ; then, with a gesture of disappointment, he turned towards the room. His gaze had fallen on a little, typical Kuresaare yard, one of the many which opened out between the stuccoed, steep-roofed houses skirting the ruined fort like the song birds, full of life and chirruping, cluster round the nest of the eagle-owl. He had looked down upon it all, vegetable-patches, hens picking on a refuse heap, a cock standing on one leg, a horse champing its bit. It had not escaped his notice that one hen mothered three ducklings among her chickens, he had seen at a glance the black and yellow down on their bodies and their waddling walk. How they must long for the water, he had thought, rising on his toes as if to get a glimpse of something on the distant horizon beyond the roofs, where the air quivered in the heat as behind a dim veil of glass. A thirst for what he could not see, yearning and disappointed, the pupils of his eyes expanded, his whole body called for salt after weeks of flavourless bread and water. The air was suffocating, and what little streamed through the crack in the window-frame seemed insipid, full of whirling atoms of dust. The sea remained invisible—far away behind the entrenchments and sand dunes.

He saw it in his mind—not the smooth sand for summer visitors at Kuresaare, but the wide, lonely sand-flats of the Kihelkonna shore. So clearly did it arise before him that he seemed to smell the rotting seaweed cast ashore by the sea, and to feel the crunching of little rosy seashells beneath his boots. He saw himself wading in the water, which slowly deepened—in calm, translucent water, at the bottom of which he could see the seaweed covering the rocks wave slowly in the current, and a swarm of tiny fish

darting away at his approach. The water rose
slowly, penetrated the tops of his high boots,
saturating his trousers, rising towards his waist.
. . . And then he was on board his boat anchored
at the edge of the shallows. Did he not hear
where he stood the restless creak of the rigging,
the ceaseless beat of the waves driven against the
stern by a favouring wind? But the boat lay
immovable, the anchor clutched the white sand
with its curved flukes, the sails drooped along
the masts and the ships' sides were mirrored in
the water. . . .

It must be gone—to-morrow—the day after
—next week it must be in Memel. . . . His
grim features become restless, his lips deep hidden
in his beard no longer twitch with ready humour.
His eyes glare like those of a beast of prey—
behind his brow his wits are at work—he cudgels
his brain striving to find a plan . . . he must
be set free this time. . . . That is the haven
towards which he must fight his way. He must
be as sure, as certain of himself, as when he
steered his smuggler's craft past hidden rocks
and watchful coastguards.

The blind alley in which he is vainly groping
becomes unbearable, he turns again to the lads
whom chance has given him for companions,

and in their curious eyes he reads the thought that fills his own mind ; they are wondering will he escape imprisonment this time or no ?

" Brushwood thieves," he grinned contemptuously at them, drawing himself up sharply to his full height, so that his broad shoulders seemed to support his body like a spar on which all else was hung.

" Boys ahoy !—what would you say was my size ? " he said.

One of the youths, the one who had spoken earlier, smiled slyly, winking at the speaker.

" Too big to be held by these walls, anyhow."

" Right," he thundered in pleasure.

" We were playing ' durak ' for thy luck," the youth went on growing bolder.

" I need no luck but my own," he answered, with head thrown back.

" They say the judge is a new one—come lately from the Mainland," the other lad put in hurriedly, anxious for a say in the matter.

Parbu-Jaan looked at the last speaker's long face, at his forehead hidden by the thick hair, at the bony contours of his nose and jaw.

" Whose boy art thou ? " he asked with an attempt of good humour. " A new judge," he added thoughtfully, already forgetting the boy.

143

" Tare Tiiu's."

" Tiiu's . . . Tiiu's," repeated Parbu-Jaan mechanically.

He began to walk excitedly to and fro. A new judge ! What if he should be able to repeat his old trick. . . . But it was too well known . . . the walls of every tavern in Saaremaa had heard it, the very foreſts had echoed it. . . . He was surprised himself now at his own daring, admiration for himself grew within him as for a ſtranger. . . . Then also he had sat awaiting trial, his feet itching to be off, his vessel eager for departure. It was then that he shut his lips to a narrow line, took on an expression grave as of one in a church and asked to be allowed to speak to the judge : " Merciful Judge-Lord, the wife is welcoming a little ſtranger—ale ought to be brewed, and then the baptism—couldn't I go for a couple of weeks ? " The judge hesitated—an old rascal, that Parbu-Jaan—but in the end consented. " See that you are back here in two weeks' time." He had raced to the Kihel-konna shore, hoiſted sail, flown off to Memel for a load of rum and gunpowder. On the day agreed he had knocked at the prison door.

His thoughts returned to those old days, as if to gather ſtrength from them. And in spite

144

of his present plight laughter shook his frame, laughter that would free his spirit and restore his pride.

Memories tossed him up and down like a vessel tossed by the waves, tormenting and provoking him to laughter. This much he knew, that never would he be able to store too many such memories. He felt his craving for new adventures to string on to the old could never be slaked. He knew that never would he be himself again until he felt the deck planks sway again beneath his feet, with his hand upon the tiller.

An autumn evening, the land showing as a dark streak, looming up strange and unfriendly even for him, as he steers towards it. The moon unnaturally large, a rent torn in the sky, gleaming dimly instead of casting light. He can hardly trust his eyes, the spray clouds his sight as with a curtain of mist ; as a rope creaks or taps against the mast he starts. He feels that the darkness that cloaks the shore is hiding something hostile, a danger of which his senses do not grasp but only some occult instinct. Suddenly, signal lights flare up on the shore . . . the coastguards ! With his comrades he begins to throw barrels overboard, grimly watching them as they roll into the water and sink—everything overboard. Next

his eyes take in the shore, marking trees, rocks
and sand-flats in the dim darkness, drawing the
place, its distance from the shore more clearly in
his memory than ever did surveyor on paper.
The following day they lift the barrels from the
bed of the sea with hooks.

Blood mingles in his memories, the sky glows
an ominous red, he sees a hand clutch the gunwale of his boat, a large browned hand with
knuckles and nails of iron—a hand whose owner
is nothing to him—a hand rising from the depths
to prevent his journey. His anger concentrates
on the hand that dares to delay his boat, to him
the hand is a living entity separated from all
body. His hatchet swings through the air and
the hand falls into the sea.

From this whirlpool his thoughts turn rapidly.
Instead he sees a bright summer day, a smooth
sea with flying gulls gleaming silver in the sunshine. He stands leaning against the mast of
his boat, cunning, reserved, following with his
eyes the Custom officials who search his vessel,
running around like rats, nosing everywhere from
hold to cabin, from cabin to deck. Without
moving a finger he watches them, casting biting
remarks at them between puffs at his pipe,
advising them of secret hiding places unknown

to them. One after the other, they crawl on
deck, discomfited as though suddenly drenched
with water and he bids a polite good-bye to their
chief, offering him a drink from his flask, bidding
him welcome another time. But as the Customs
boat grates on the sand, he seizes the coil of rope
on which one of the searchers had sat, and between
his hands rubs its end, which crumbles into brown
leaves with a familiar smell—a twisted rope of
tobacco.

Again he cast a yearning glance through the
window. It is the middle of August, at nights
the sky gleams with stars, each one a compass.
It is his pride to sail to Memel or the Swedish
coast without a compass, trusting only to these
tiny guides, which through the night vanish,
light up and shift as the yawl sails on.

" Was't thou who said there is a new judge ? "
he asked suddenly, turning to the boys.

" It was I," one of the boys replied, proud of
his knowledge.

Parbu-Jaan smiled, his hand stroking meanwhile his beard. In his fancy he heard the sound
of words and much talk, his own voice rising and
gaining confidence, some one laughing outright.
. . . His hand clenched in a tight grip. . . .
Now he has gotten the idea . . . just that. . . .

147

As yet he is not quite certain, the scheme is almost too daredevil, but he must close his eyes to the danger. His state of mind is that of a diver in deep water ; perhaps he may sink for ever, more likely he will rise again to the surface.

He looked at the boys and began already to play his new part—his keen, knowing eyes dilated and became vacant and stupid, his shoulders drooped, his hair fell over his forehead, hiding its strong intelligent lines, the firm decision of his mouth is lost in loose, gaping lips.

" Well, whom do I look like now ? " he asked, turning to the two youths and pushing his cap to the back of his head.

They stared at him startled, something of wild savagery had suddenly come over him, something terrifying and inexplicable ; they looked questioningly at each other, perplexed and open mouthed.

" Like Mad-Mats," whispered one into the other's ear.

" Right, boys. I am not quite right in my head, remember that. All night I have talked gibberish, I can no longer tell the moon from the sun. . . . If any one asks, say that."

The shifty eyes of the elder youth flashed and expanded, gleaming with understanding and

148

admiration. The other stared, uncomprehending.

The elder youth bent suddenly towards Parbu-Jaan.

" What wilt thou give us ? " he whispered.

Parbu-Jaan eyed him sternly, and broke into a laugh ; he felt as proud of the boy as though he himself had trained him, the lad's early-developed business sense appealed to his own instincts.

" A gun and powder, of the best make," he threw the words hastily at him as the warder's steps sounded in the corridor. The boy threw himself with his whole weight against the door, and beat on it with his fists.

The startled eyes of the warder appeared in the spy-hole, eyes used to darkness which appeared perpetually to dread any disturbance of the every-day round.

" What has happened here ? " he said in a chiding tone, as though reprimanding a child.

Parbu-Jaan stood in a corner, muttering to himself. The youths had drawn as far as possible away from him.

" We want to be put in another cell," cried the elder youth. " We can't stand him—he isn't right here, all night we got no peace listening

to him talk, talk, talk as fast as his tongue would
let him."

The warder looked suspiciously at Parbu-Jaan.

" What has happened to him here ? " he grum-
bled. For his own part, he would have been
ready to let them all go, guilty and innocent alike,
but being set to guard them, what could he
do ?

" What has addled his wits now ? " he repeated
to himself.

" Let us go to the judge," he said quietly and
coaxingly as to a naughty child, laying his hand
gently on Parbu-Jaan's shoulder and pushing him
out of the room.

Parbu-Jaan obeyed without resisting, not for
a moment forgetting his part, his lips moving
all the while in babble of meaningless words.

In the court-room the judge, a bespectacled
gentleman, waited with his clerk.

" This man has gone mad during the night,"
the warder humbly explained, as though the
misfortune was partly his fault.

The judge cast a cold eye on Parbu-Jaan, and
despite its coldness, Parbu-Jaan felt himself go
hot.

" That remains to be seen," the judge said
dryly.

He read the charge in a loud voice, Parbu-Jaan listening with his eyes wandering uneasily round the room.

"Two empty coffee-sacks stamped with the Memel seal were found in the attic of Parbu's house," the judge finished his charge.

"Well, look now—don't lies get found out, gracious Judge-Lord," said Parbu-Jaan. "Sacks! As though coffee was ever carried in a sack— why, it would drip out."

"What nonsense art thou talking?" said the judge.

"Only that no one carries coffee in a sack— coffee's a drink."

"Dost thou not know coffee, man?"

"How should I know gentlefolks' dainties?"

The judge looked at him for a while and then said:

"Come here—is not this thy compass?"

Parbu-Jaan reeled towards the table, purposely dragging his feet. With head on one side, he began to examine the compass.

"Well now, isn't that queer? It's moving —well, by . . . it's dancing like anything, what's the matter with it?"

"Man, remember with whom thou speakest. Who am I?"

"Thou art one of God's errand boys. When God draws up the laws on the tables of stone, thou bringest them down to us."

"Man, where wert thou last week?"

"I sat in the threshing-barn as God had created me, the wife washing my only shirt."

"Confessest thou or not?"

"Of course I confess whatever the Judge-Lord wishes. To everything I say only yea and amen."

"Thou wert then in Memel?"

"Certainly."

"When did that occur?"

"It is hardly twenty years ago."

"Have a care what you say, man."

"That is what I'm doing, and a care for my back too. I am not altogether mad, though not so clever as your Honour."

"Pah! I have no time for lunatics."

Parbu-Jaan's head drooped lower, and a smile vanished in his bushy beard. He dragged himself after the warder out of the court, the warder staring at him with respect mingled with fear. In the prison yard he paused—looked up at a window to where two youthful heads gazed curiously down at him, and waved his hand with a toss of his skipper's beard. His nostrils dilated as though the scent of the sea had struck them.

Six hours later he was bound for Memel, in the bright moonshine of an August night—with thousands of tiny, winking stars for a compass.

Alien Blood

HER NAME WAS REET, AND SHE
was as fresh and pure-blooded an island
girl as you could wish to see, from the village
of Sõrve Säär, in the southern half of the Island
of Saaremaa. Her father was Treiali-Jaan, a
white-bearded man of stalwart frame, who limped
slightly with the foot he had injured in the seal-
hunting; her mother Panga-Tiiu, from the same
village. In addition, her grandparents, both
on her father's and mother's side, were, if not
from the same village, at least from the same
parish of Jämaja, or at the farthest, from one of the
adjoining parishes of Ansiküla and Kihelkonna.

Cape Sõrve Säär does justice to its name,[1]
prolonging as it does the length of Saaremaa
by thirty versts and stretching out far into the
sea towards the homes of the Livs, towards
Domesnaes in Courland, to which its tide-covered
sand-flats seem to extend a tentative greeting.
Before its final dive into the sea it winds and
wriggles for a verst or so, looking like the yellow
belly of some huge sea-monster floating on its
back, till it narrows at last to a resting-place for
seagulls only.

[1] The word " Säär " means a leg.

Sõrve has always lain hidden from the sight of God. In earlier times it was separated from the rest of Saaremaa by a creek called Salmejõgi, made with a single stroke of his knife by Suur-Töll, an island giant ; now one crosses dryshod the channel of what once was a stream. Even to-day, the smuggler who gains the shelter of the forests in farthest Sõrve is safe ; there he is unseen even of God.

The sea round Säär is treacherous and full of reefs : a veritable cemetery of ships. As far back as the memories of men can reach it has drawn down ships to destruction, almost every year. A beacon winking an intermittent light, a lifeboat station and a watchhouse of the coastguard stood on the kneecap of Säär until the first years of world-war, when the shells from German warships wiped them off the face of the earth, together with half the village.

In spite of beacons, however, the old law had endured from the middle ages, framed for the fishermen of this same Sõrve, threatening all wreckers and robbers of the coast with dismissal from the Church's table and commanding their bodies to be cast into the sea at the place where they had sinned " against the Lord of Land and Sea and against all true believers," while the savers of shipwrecked mariners were promised absolution for the period of one year and forty days.

Along the sandy belt of Sõrve Säär, Treiali-Reet was wont to trip as a tiny maiden like the sea-birds, farther and ſtill farther, until the foam drove soft between her toes, and the sandy belt was loſt in the wide expanse of blue. Only then did Reet ſtop, on the uttermoſt spit, with two seas, the Swedish Sea and the Lõpemeri, joining in ripples over her feet.

From her childhood Reet was a true example of Sõrve maidenhood, with a black skirt beginning at her armpits and pleated into folds that ended in a ſtriped hem of white and red—a skirt that had lain in a baking-oven according to the Sõrve cuſtom, to preserve its folds, a red ſtocking-cap on her head, with a tassel that tried to outdance her flaxen locks in the wind. From afar she looked like a little red-capped, fly-agaric mushroom.

Her childhood sped by on the open, lonely shore, where almoſt every house in the village had its own windmill, ſtanding on its base of rocks. She grew up among forsaken boats rotting on the reefs, lying with sides prized off for use elsewhere and looking like great skeletons with greenish ribs, between which flickered tiny codfish and young sprats. She gathered pebbles on the beach, some of which bore marks of ancient snails and crustaceans, while others were porous like petrified sponges.

In the spring the dead bodies of migratory birds lay each morning at the foot of the lighthouse, their tiny skulls shattered against the treacherous lantern, that had lured the wanderers returning from distant lands to their breeding-places on the rocks and reefs of Saaremaa. Reet mourned bitterly the death of these strangers from afar and to her their fate seemed pitiable, but the lighthouse-keeper was more matter-of-fact : he chose the eatable among them, filled his pan and cooked them for food.

Treiali-Jaan, Reet's father, and Poleühtid, his brother-in-law, both belonged to the lifeboat crew. Poleühtid was a lantern-jawed bachelor with a seaman's beard, who had spent the year of his manhood sailing in foreign vessels. Rumour had obstinately attempted to stamp him a leper, but Poleühtid had allowed two witnesses to examine his body in the bath, and thereafter threatened to break two ribs of any one who still dared to call him leprous ; after which he was left in peace. He lived with his brother-in-law ; whenever the gun at the lifeboat station boomed, they were expected to be each at his oar in the lifeboat within a quarter of an hour, together with six other of the villagers, whatever Devil's weather was afoot. Their oilskins and capes hung waiting in the boat-shed.

After stormy nights, the dawn that followed would show a striking sight on the shore of Säär : the water would be filled with seaweed, wrenched free by the waves and lying in long, dark-brown fringes along the yellow line of sand, and with floating cargo. The whole population of the village, men, women and girls would be afoot, and the work of salving in full swing. Thus it had been hundreds of years ago on the shore of Sõrve Säär, and thus it was to-day. It was a species of catch that never failed. The sea gave everything, driftwood, the wreckage of ships, precious booty. After a few days, long lines of carts would be strung out towards Kuresaare. And according to the law, one-fourth of the find belonged to the salver if it had been taken up within a verst from the shore, and one-sixth should the distance have been over one verst.

These were days of rejoicing, life around the lighthouse in the village of Sõrve Säär being otherwise monotonous and lonely. Kuresaare, the only town on the island, lay over forty versts away. During the summers, only the women, children and the aged were at home; during the autumns, however, when the men had returned from their voyages, the music of bagpipes and accordions was heard in the evenings, and weddings were celebrated, now that time allowed, in batches, as many as fifteen at the same time. Home-brewed ale of malt and wild rosemary was made; mixed with spirits and honey it soon bowled a man over. The whole village caroused for a few weeks; and then came the winter's sleep when the sea was frozen over, and in the spring cradles were brought out in the houses on the Säär.

In this manner, life went by on Sõrve Säär.

And thus would the life of young Treiali-Reet have been had not her fate been written otherwise in the stars.

Reet had reached the age of twenty. Her storehouse contained seven dresses of the Sõrve style, all spun by herself, a black, yellow-edged mourning-dress formed an eighth, coloured vests and stocking-caps were there, enough for many years, and an ornamented chest painted red was full of stockings and mittens.

Like a true Sõrve woman, she carried out the

work of a man during the summer, ploughed the potato-field, ever threatened by the flying sand, with a wooden plough, but instead of withering her, the hard work seemed to increase her healthy island beauty. Under the breath of sea winds she bloomed full-blooded. Her hair, smoothed down on Sundays with butter, was of the colour of the golden sand, her hands and feet were small, her hips generous, her chin showed an alluring dimple.

She had never been outside of her own island and her visits to Kuresaare were easily counted. In the autumns she danced at all the weddings that were celebrated on Säär, but of her own wedding nothing had as yet been spoken. She seemed in no hurry to be married, and her mother, Tiiu, accused her of waiting for a junk-dealer for a husband.

Then one summer came the great storm from the north-east, of which the coast-dwellers of Sõrve still speak years afterwards. The men were out the whole night. At dawn the sea was rolling savage and tawny under a sky rent by the winds, and part of the sandspit had vanished beneath the waves ; a great foreign vessel had been shipwrecked on the Swedish Sea, near Säär.

Treiali-Jaan and Poleühtid brought ashore with them, in a boat filled down to the water's edge with salved coffee-sacks, a man whom they had found floating on a plank.

The man had swallowed much sea-water and was otherwise bruised and broken ; he was placed in the back bed of the Treiali's hut, where he lay silent as a piece of driftwood.

He was of medium height, stockily built, his hair black as pitch, his body brown and his arms tatooed with blue anchors. His teeth were locked so tightly that they had to be forced open with a piece of wood before spirits could be poured down his throat.

Treiali-Reet was put to nurse him. She sat beside the bed with her knitting in her hand, a thing never left aside by a true Sõrve maiden even in her dreams, and moving her needles looked at him. Never had she seen anything as dark as this man's hair was. It was so black that it seemed to shimmer with green, like the tail feathers of a cock.

The man's hands moved as though he sought something. Reet followed the fumbling movement of the fingers, and seeing a band hung round his neck drew out from under his shirt a square piece of red cloth. As soon as she had placed this in his hands, they rested quietly again, shutting tightly round the piece of cloth.

On the third day he began to speak. But it was in a most strange, sing-song language which nobody understood. It was neither German nor Russian, nor was it English, said Poleühtid.

Then he began to gesticulate with his fingers, which moved more quickly than his tongue, as though each separate finger had spoken its own language.

Reet helped him into a sitting posture, pointed to the sea outside, then to the man himself, and shook her head.

She understood that he wished for news of his comrades and the ship that had borne him, and it was a relief to her when he sunk again into a torpor.

The following day found the man on his feet. He shook himself like a dog risen from the water, stretched himself and nothing seemed the matter with him. He followed Reet when she went to the shore to clean fish and from there to the wash-tub. He never left her for a moment, following after when she went to the cattle-yard and from the cattle-yard to the well.

The Russian lighthouse-keeper came to interview him and to demand his passport, but the man turned his pockets inside out and the matter was left at that.

Treiali-Jaan had departed the day before with a sailing-boat to Hiiumaa, and of the men only Poleühtid was at home. In the evening, when Poleühtid went according to his habit to smoke near the large osier fish-traps on the shore, he fancied he saw two shadows behind a fishing-boat, that merged together on the sand. He moved his pipe thoughtfully to the other corner of his mouth ; he had his own idea of what he had seen.

Still the same evening he wandered over to the harbour to inquire after boats bound for Riga or Windau and made an agreement with old Eitea that he should take the stranger to the Courland coast as soon as a favourable wind occurred.

Having done this, Poleühtid rested. Passing the door of the outbuilding that was Reet's room, he tried the door as though by accident, but it was closed on the inside and everything was quiet, from the motionless wings of the windmills to the fish-traps that lay sleeping with mouths agape.

When Poleühtid tried next morning to explain to the stranger by signs his coming journey, Reet stood stirring the potato-broth in a cauldron hanging from a hook over the open fireplace.

163

And in spite of the glow from the fire, her young, ruddy face suddenly paled, almost to the colour of the Saaremaa limestone rocks, as though her heart had drawn up all the blood into itself like a sponge.

She sat down for a space on the sooty hearth-stone, spoke not a word ; then, taking the broth from the fire, went to her outbuilding.

There it was cool and only half-lighted. From the rafters hung the dresses she herself had spun, the dowry she had spent years in making.

Everything would be as before, the village of Säär and the windmills, the rotting boats on the shore, and each autumn the weddings to the accompaniment of the bagpipes.

And she, the daughter of Treiali-Jaan and the niece of Poleühtid, she would marry one of the villagers, as all the friends of her girlhood had done and her ancestors before her.

But the stranger she would never see, never until the bells rang for the resurrection and the bones scattered here and there called to one another.

In the evening the aged Eitea came to report that the ship " Berta " was ready to sail and that the wind was rising in the north-east ; the follow-

ing morning, at the peep of dawn, she would start
on her voyage.

The stranger sat on the edge of his bed and
smeared his topboots with seal-fat ; he seemed
to understand what the question was about.

Drawing the boots on his feet he went down
to the shore, a moment later followed by Reet,
who crept out of the hut. They met near the
large osier fish-trap ; the sea was all rippling
wavelets, all the windmills in the village were at
work.

As though by common agreement they started
to walk away along the shore, sinking in the
loose sand at each step, and soon the village lay
far behind them.

They walked close to each other, each with an
arm round the other's waist, clinging tightly
together.

Farther along the shore they found a boat and
rowed out to sea. Reet rowed, as all island women
do, and the stranger sat in the stern.

A couple of versts away they disembarked on
an open shore where only coarse sedge grew.
It was covered with the empty nests of seabirds
and at each step they trod on broken egg-shells.
Some animal of the mole tribe had burrowed the
whole land hollow and the sand-hills were full of

little holes.   An invisible shore-pink spread its perfume from some hiding-place in the sedge or the sand-hills.

A flock of wild geese rose up in the air at their approach.

The sun went down—departed to the home of the gods.

And there, in the coarse sedge, with the gulls shrieking above their heads, they lived through the hour of parting.

The following morning the stranger went his way, and Eitea took him with his ship " Berta " to Courland.

He never came back.   But nine months later Treiali-Reet gave birth to a son who had black hair and a brown skin.

She moved later with her boy from the village of Säär to another village, still more distant from the world and still more secluded.   By her work she earned food for them both, and later her son worked for her.

She was calm and without fear, like one who has taken her share of life and has no further desires.   Her son grew to be a good seaman, and in his turn brought into the world many children, all dark-complexioned as he was.   His descendants still live in the same village, ever distinct from their fair-skinned neighbours. As sailors they are the best of the island, living on the water from their childhood like young sea-birds.

And thus Treiali-Reet became the fore-mother of a dark-skinned race in whose veins there throbbed a hotter, bolder blood calling them to distant seas and ventures.

The Rye-Field

THE END OF JURNAS KARHEIDING'S cigarette glowed like a burning spot of red through the dusk :

" A ripening rye-field with thousands and thousands of nodding ears, awaiting a common fate, their stems bending and breaking in unison, the still soft grain with its first faint hint of the scent of bread, the Estonian blue of the corn-flower. For me, all these are inseparably con-nected with a certain memory.

" It is long since then. I had matriculated at the University the previous spring, studying at first theology according to my father's desire, only to go later over to jurisprudence. I was an ordinary Estonian peasant-undergraduate, in outward appearance at least, my coat of coarse striped homespun, the work of a village tailor, the trousers too short, socks,—well, the type is familiar to you. Inwardly I was still nebulous, a burning chaos of whirling atoms striving to-wards order, filled with a belief that the creation of brand-new worlds was to be my lot. On the other hand, my nerves were as quivering, as tautly-strung, as silken-fine as those of any French Marquis before the great catastrophe.

" In this ſtate I arrived to enjoy my first under
graduate summer vacation at the home farm.
My home was in North Livland twenty or so
verſts from Tartu. You all know this Livland
landscape, the clover-fields and a few sudden
tiny pink¦ patches of buckwheat between the
rye and the home-grown wheat, flax in plenty,
growing more conspicuous as one approaches
Viljandi. Little lazy brooks shadowed by silver
willow, water-lily pools, spruce-woods, turf-bogs,
manors with their orchards, Eſtonian peasant
farms. A fertile fruitful land, a second Denmark.
The odour of golden ball, branches of flowering
mezereon, poisonously scented as the perfume
of a courtesan, a moon draped in a red cloud.

" Immediately on my arrival, I fell in love,
fathomless, hopeless love. I sank at once as
one drowning in a whirlpool. The objeĉt of
my love was the wife of the foreſter on the neighbouring manor, a woman ten years older than
I, but ſtill young, a delightful being, blonde, a
keen horsewoman, ears small, like rosy shells, a
high forehead arching backward, fine quivering
noſtrils, a wealth of golden-red hair like a field
of ripe wheat crowning her brow. What her
charaĉter was otherwise, whether good or bad,
intelligent, sensuous, vain or passionate, I neither

169

knew nor cared. For me she was Woman. In her all secrets lay buried, the burning problem of my own young blood among them.

" That she was married, that she had a husband and children, seemed only natural to me ; in no way did this disturb my love. Towards her husband I even felt a kind of good-will, not quite without a sense of superiority. He was one of those silent, good-natured, pale-faced men, slow and gentle in his movements for all the professional forester he was,—his hair always too long in the neck, a matter which, the Lord knows why, invested him with a peculiarly humble air in my eyes. Each time I met him in the company of his wife I saw him watch the strange, sensitive and dangerous quivering of those nostrils, more eloquent than words by far, meekly and with a kind of inward dejection.

" Many visitors came to the forester's house, and among these was the tenant of the adjoining manor, an Estonian called Ibrus, a strongly-built, dark-blooded man with a gleaming beard, always attired in shooting-boots, and in his hat a waving green-black cock's feather. From the beginning, I took an instinctive dislike to him, such as only individuals of the same sex may feel to one another. And yet he was regarded everywhere as a pleasant, in many things excellent, man ; he had many of the qualities that breed popularity. He could relate anecdotes so that his hearers writhed with laughter, and they were never coarse ; his conduct towards women combined the right proportions of chivalry, irony and protective manliness, a combination which no woman could resist ; further, he was attentive to both old and young. To me he was distasteful in just this, in his capacity of a man, as a sexual being, probably in some degree on account of his all-conquering attraction for women, but chiefly because he was commonly spoken of as the lover of the forester's beautiful wife.

" This suspicion, for I had no real proof, could not lessen my love for her, but the contrary. From the beginning I was aware of the hopelessness of my love, but was willing, nay, keenly eager to suffer, suffering being an essential ingredient in my love. But another desire developed slowly and resistlessly in me : I wanted to see the two together, I wanted to surprise them. And to this day I cannot say what the motive power behind this constant, all-devouring desire was, whether it was the wish to exalt my suffering to its highest pitch, or merely my dislike for Ibrus.

" I began, therefore, to spy on them always and everywhere, with a fertility of invention and an untiring energy that surprised even myself. My watching was rendered easier by the fact that the manor within which the forester's dwelling stood was distant only a few kilometres from that rented by Ibrus, my father's farm lying about midway between them. I recollect many nights when dawn found me on the look-out for them in the garden of one or other of the manors, I recall silent night watches in orchards fully dark only at midnight, beneath lichen-covered apple and cherry trees, where I crouched waiting for a light to twinkle at some window. Dawn came and the morning lived around me, bright Livland mornings ; hens and cocks awoke from their brief torpor in the barns of the manors, the pigeons left their dove-cots, the bees began their humming about my head. My feet turned cold in the dew-drenched grass, and my clothes were covered by gleaming cobwebs, dotted with dew-drops.

" On such mornings my father would scold me for running after maidens.

" 'You are beginning early, young jackanapes,' he said.

" And I allowed him to remain in this belief.

" The most mortifying of these memories is one of a wait of four hours in the yard of an hotel in the adjacent town. I sat in the hay in my father's cart, having come ostensibly on his business, but really because I had heard she had gone off to town. I knew that she was staying at this hotel, somewhere behind the windows already darkened, which seemed to look down at me with an evil stare.

" I crouched in the cart, shivering, and two stars appeared in the narrow strip of sky visible from the shed, which smelled of manure and chopped straw. At that moment I loved her beyond words, breath failed me at the thought of her. Often I pictured her in my mind, her magnificent hair piled up on her head, her sun-burned throat and high bosom with its covering of white blouse, the strong arms gleaming rosy through her sleeves. A porter crossed the yard carrying a lantern and opened the iron-shod door for a peasant who drove in. It began to rain and all became damp, mournful and still darker around me ; an unpleasant smell of rotting straw assailed my nostrils, but she came not. She came not. . . . And what could I have done or even said if suddenly she had appeared . . . ? I should have crouched deeper in the sheltering

hay beneath my gaudy horse-blanket, and listened
to the rustle of her skirts as she went by, savouring
the exquisite pain of finding her unfaithful. . . .
But she came not. . . . Maybe I had mistaken
the place, likely also at the last moment she had
put off her journey. Anyhow, she never came,
and at last I had to start for home with my mission
unfulfilled the heavy creaking gate opened to me
also, my springless cart jolted out into the badly-
paved street.

"But once I was to entrap them. And it
happened in this manner :

" I had seen them set out together for a walk,
in brightest daylight, along the lane, in the sight
of all, so careless or so blindly infatuated were
they. Keeping well behind, I crept after them
along the edge of a field, without losing sight of
them for a moment, seeing the whole time her
green sunshade, beside which all other greens,
the leaves of trees, the very grass seemed pale
and colourless.

" Suddenly, they disappeared among the rye,
growing to the height of a man in a field as yet
unreaped. The rye closed behind them, the
thousands and thousands of stems joining together like a protecting wall around their love.

" They were trapped irretrievably,—delivered

into my power. In my hands I held their fate.

" I caſt myself down on the clover, left to seed. Beside me the rye-field gently billowed, ripe for cutting, larks shot into the sky, but without song.

" I thought of my revenge, of the faċt that I had them in my grasp. To escape unnoticed from the field she would have to transform herself into one of the red-mottled butterflies that floated lazily and lingeringly over the rye.

" I thought of how her noſtrils quivered and lived, of how she smelled sweet as the young grass and the cornflowers she passed, scented as the clover over-blown and over-ripe on which I lay.

" For the firſt time awoke in me foreboding of what love meant. Not love such as mine, not the torturing fire that burned in my blood, but the passion of those two in the rye-field.

" How infinitely happy they were—finite, doomed, vanishing human atoms.

" And juſt then the foreſter appeared at the edge of the spruce-wood. Even now I can see him, his colourless, melancholy eyes in which pain and doubt burned together, his over-long hair and the ſtubby growth on his cheeks. His clothes were covered with spruce-needles.

" Something rapturous awoke in me. Revenge fell right into my lap. I was at that moment the keeper of the fate of three souls.

" The forester approached me.

" ' Young man,' he said, ' have you seen my wife ? '

" Then,—well—then—I answered him :

" ' Yes. I saw her a while ago go along yonder forest path.   She was alone.'

" He breathed a sigh of relief and turned in the direction I had pointed.   His hair uncut at the neck, his gait that of a weary and unhappy man.

" But I rose and crept away into the forest, and there lay down on the edge of a pool, breaking with both hands the wild rosemary, and not returning home till midnight had come."

A Love Story

EVERYTHING IS NOW LONG OVER, eighty has claimed me for its own, my fingers are distorted by the gout, legs aching however often they are bled—the earth beginning to call me to rest.

Of my childhood there is little to say, why should I dwell on it, the childhood of the poor. Only my mother was unnaturally strict—whether hardened by excess of work or of her nature severe, it is not for me to say. Once in the twilight I was given the key of the hut to carry as we came from some visit, and in pastime I swung it between my finger-tips until it fell into the grass and was lost there as though the earth had swallowed it. It was sought after with a lantern, even, but it was not to be found. And then my mother beat me with a branch of juniper, me a big girl, until I was almost crippled. Resentment filled me from that hour and I could not forget. If she had only taken a birch-rod ! My father was, on the other hand, an extremely good man and never laid hands on us children, excepting a rap, perhaps, on the head with his last or with the edge of a boot when we passed him in the winter sitting at his cobbling.

At sixteen, I had to leave home, my brothers having already gone to sea. I was hired to a middling sized farm in the same parish. There I served for two years, and grew up to womanhood, also in due course partook of my first communion while still working in my situation. All work allotted to me I did, minding the children, feeding the cows and working in the fields, in short, anything, never complaining of overwork. My wages were paid in cloth, a woollen dress, linen for underclothing and two pairs of boots, and later, ten roubles in money were added. I was not strikingly beautiful or in any manner out of the way, an ordinary girl, only that my hair grew so profusely that I hardly knew how to coil it, the weight of my plait giving me headaches. I was a merry girl and in every way companionable, people having always shown fondness for me and sought my company. I have myself wondered at it, not being inclined to bow down before others or to flatter, though neither do I speak evil of any one behind his back.

Such being the case, what was to prevent me from living, neither sorrows nor my years weighing on me ; I was at all the village dances and at the big swing, like any child of the world ; only

178

the rowdy ones I could not bear, refusing to join their company.

In the autumn a new farm hand from the Parish of Kärla was taken on, called Laur, quick with his hands, honest in nature, a manly fellow. I suppose it was fate. Each soon found favour in the other's sight, and we began to seek each other's company, as is the fashion of the young, so that we were together at the dances and at the fair at Kuresaare town. Only I would never let him come to my loft, though he begged me often to, even getting angry when I said no.

People began to tease us and regard us as betrothed, nor did we deny it ; matters being so, what would have been the use ? On Candlemas Day Laur brought me a ring from town— here it is still beside my gout-ring—and a silken shawl with large flowers. We began to inquire after a site for a hut on the manor, but still put off the wedding, both being yet young and poor.

And in this way love took such deep root in our hearts that only death can free us from it.

But God salts the cake of each of us according to His will.

The vicar began to want Laur for his coachman and thus Laur came to the manse, ten versts from the farm where I served. And there it happened. The vicar had a maid-servant called Epp, a couple of years older than Laur, short-necked, stoutish,—however it may have happened, she bore Laur a child. In some manner they erred, being always together and the flesh weak and sin sweet.

When I heard of it, and that was soon enough, my heart became hard, as hard as stone. Young as I was and hot blooded, I refused to see Laur, returning his letters and hating Epp, slandering her and calling her by ugly names. Who knows whether I might not have relented with time and all turned to the best, had not the vicar meddled in the matter and begun to demand that Laur should marry Epp. There it was. What was a farm hand to do, the authorities were not to be moved, the sin had been committed, and in addition it was the vicar's own servant. No words were wasted, the banns were put up and the wedding celebrated on the same day as the baptism.

But for me hard times began. Who knows? Perhaps we were all alike, or had I become more sensitive than others? All I know is that the blow struck deep. I became as though half-witted, quite ill, lying for many weeks in constant pain. Once they believed I was dead and had already placed a hymnbook on my breast and sung the hymn for those dead, but at the Lord's Prayer I opened my eyes again. My hair fell out altogether after the illness, filling the comb at each draw as hay clings to a rake, only a short pigtail remaining at the back of my head. I gathered the fallen hair and had a plait made of it at Kuresaare—for a keepsake. And as soon as I could move about, I left the neighbourhood altogether, taking a situation at the chemist's at Kuresaare.

There, among strangers, life was easier. But one day, just as I was cleaning fish for dinner on the steps, I saw Laur enter the yard from the gate. I pretended not to see him, only the knife moved faster in my hand so that the fish-scales flew about me.

Laur came quite close, to the foot of the steps, and without wishing me good-day, went right to the gist of the matter : " Maret, are you angry with me ? "

My heart beat hard at this question, but I only said : " Why do you ask me ?—if you have anything else to say, my good man, say it. Why don't you go to your wife, you have your Epp, what have I to do with you ? "

Laur said again, looking at me from the foot of the steps :

" I have loved only you, Maret, and now you know it."

At that my blood boiled again, the old Adam rising in me, and going in, I sought the plait from its hiding, the hair I had lost in my illness, and taking it to the door showed it to him, taking at the same time the shawl from my sparse locks.

" Thus have I mourned you," I said. " But go now in peace and may happiness follow you in all your actions."

" Maret," said Laur, without a movement to go, " I have done wrong, I know. Do you no longer care at all for me ? "

This angered me again and I answered :

" It is a sin and a shame for the husband of another woman to come and say what may not be said. Let this be the last time you show yourself here."

I wiped the fish-scales from my hands, went in again and brought out the ring and the silken shawl.

" Here,—take back what is yours," I said.

" I will not take them,—they are yours," he said, red in the face, as though with rage.

I put them on the steps and went indoors then, taking the fish with me and not glancing behind.

He went, and I noticed afterwards that he had taken the ring and the silk with him. Once again he sent word by a boy that I was to meet him on Sunday at the church, near the sacristy. I never went and sent no answer.

And with that he was gone. Gone without coming back. I never sent for him and he never came.

But how is one to escape one's longings and one's love?

Our longing is such that it stretches out as though on a thread, for miles without end.

The days pass quickly enough with work and bustle, too much so for a poor maid-servant, the din of this world too much in her ears. But when night comes and you lie awake in your bed, and the night happens to be one of those summer nights which are neither night nor day, the sky one level light, then you feel in your soul that only the death can end the longing.

And this you know also, somewhere another lies awake, he too bereft of sleep, lying awake in his bed and longing for you.

Now and then I would hear of them, though

183

I never asked, there being always those willing to gossip. Some seemed to think they were doing me a service, others wanted to see my mortification, such is the nature of man. I listened always as though the talk was of strangers. Laur had left his situation as coachman and set up for himself as a farmer, living in a hut on the manor estate, though the building was their own. Another girl had been born to them in addition to the first. They lived, scraping along, after the manner of small peasants, nothing remarkable in that. Only that Laur seemed to be ailing for some time, his wife Epp having been to the chemist for medicine for pains in the chest or whatever it may have been.

A few years passed again—I still at the same chemist's—when one September day Laur's wife Epp came to see me and said :

" Laur seems to be going, wouldn't you come to see him once more ? "

A red-hot needle seemed to pierce my heart, but I was too proud to show it, least of all to Epp. So I only asked, as though of a stranger :

" Did Laur send for me ? "

Epp said, and quite humbly she spoke :

" Laur himself—how could it be otherwise."

I looked at her, my heart melting, and I

thought: you too seem to have suffered, if I have—so altered and yellow was Epp.

I went with her. Passing the baker's I dropped in and bought bread rings threaded on a string.

She had no cart, Epp, so we went on foot, the two of us. It was autumn, the mountain ash thick with berries, dogrose covered with hips lining the road. Neither Epp nor I spoke. Only once I asked :

" Has Laur been ill long ? "

To which Epp replied :

" Over two years now."

The remaining five or six versts we walked in silence. And that was the whole journey.

At Laur's hut, the elder of the two daughters came to meet us, and recognizing her from her likeness to Laur, I gave her the shortbread. Opening the door of the little chamber my heart throbbed painfully, and I nearly fell on the threshold, so nerveless were my limbs, but for Epp's sake I had to draw myself together.

I saw at once that the end was near. So completely had he altered, poor man, his cheekbones standing out, his nose sharp and narrow, the breath rattling in his chest. But at me he looked keenly, as though boring me to the wall, waving his bony hand for Epp to leave us.

As soon as we were alone, he said :

" Maret, have you forgiven me ? "

Tears gripped me by the throat, a lump so big rising in it that I could not speak, not a single word.

But the dying man still insisted :

" In the name of Jesus Christ, have you forgiven me ? "

And at that I dropped down against the bed, with the strength all fled from my body, like a skein of wool I was, and bursting into tears I said :

" I have, I have forgiven everything."

Then he closed his eyes for a moment and after a while said, with eyes still closed :

" I have loved only you, Maret."

For a while I remained on my knees near the bed, feeling that I could stay there for ever, so sweet it was—such bliss. The suffering of many years melted away in the tears I shed. I could have died there, by his side, and never missed the life still before me.

And that was all he said to me.

When I left him, he was asleep,—Epp stood in the porch, the younger child in her arms, the older eating the bread I had brought them.

" Good-bye, Epp," I said, and we shook hands.

I was about to add something about Laur, but
could not bring myself to pronounce his name,
and so I was silent.   All I knew was that there
was no grudge in my heart, neither against Epp
nor any other person.

In the night he died.   Epp came once again
to town to see me, bringing Laur's ring, saying
it had been his last wish.   I accepted it as he
had wished, but never put it on my finger until I
heard that Epp too had died, about ten years
ago.

But after Laur's death I could no longer stay
even where I was, moving away from Saaremaa
altogether to service at Tallinn, and here I have
been since then.   Never once have I visited
the island which was my home, and all are now
dead, parents, brothers and all, only a sister-in-
law being perhaps still among the living.

The worst pain lasted its time and then wore
off, leaving my heart dead, neither joy nor sorrow
any longer there.

I sought solace elsewhere, beginning to visit
Bible meetings and to study the Word of God,
and becoming converted, found true consolation.

Suitors for my hand were many—a little was
left in every year, you see, to put away in an old

stocking.   Among them was even a valet of the
Germans, and a sergeant, once, even a land-
owning farmer from the country, a widower,
with a real go-between to act for him.   The last
suitor appeared when I was already approaching
the sixties.   I sent them all away.

Now there have been none for a score of years;
all have left me in peace, a poor old cripple.   I
have my own room, my fuchsia flowering in the
window, revival meetings every summer,—and
as yet, God be thanked, no lack of bread.

But this I say and mean it, when the call comes
I shall not resist it, being ready to leave this
world and its vanities whenever God in His
wisdom sees fit.

The Stranger

MATUSHKA STOOD UNDER THE glass veranda in full Russian ceremonial attire, garbed in her eternal mourning, never once left off since the death of her only daughter, and announced that supper was ready, her cheeks faintly flushed by the mysterious task of pie-baking and by the feeling of satisfaction which accompanies hospitality.

From the garden, behind the jasmine-bushes, came the voices of Batjushka and the stranger in reply.

The unseen presence of the sea made itself felt from both sides over the garden planted in gravelly sand, as a faint salty smell, to which the flats and the grazing-moors added the scent of dried grass.

Hazel-bushes and tall chestnuts hid the lane, so that only the green cupola of the little white church stood out against a cold yellow sky.

In the air was a hint of evening and of autumn.

Amid the fading Saaremaa landscape, cherries nodding in their ripeness and bright as glass glowed against the darkening green of the trees, imparting to them touches of sensuous and luxurious colour.

Batjushka, an Estonian by birth, and wearing a white cassock that had seen many washings and was now as faded as his grey hair and beard, led his guest along the garden paths, his face lit by a smile that was gentle, tired and faded as himself.

Paul Karask alone seemed conscious of the vague beauty of the sun-parched plain shining grey in the evening light. Its spirit seemed to evade him, elusive and unyielding as he strove to analyse its mystery. Yet the beauty of it all forced itself upon him, though he lacked some one to whom he might impart the impressions that gradually were taking shape in his brain.

" Forgive the Matushka, if she begins to speak of Masha again," Batjushka said as they bent to pass under a cherry tree. " She cannot help it, it seems to unburden her heart, she is so lonely here, poor woman."

" Was your daughter's name Masha ? " the stranger absently inquired, and a couple of glassy red cherries fell on his shoulder. " Maria Alexandrovna ? " he continued, collecting himself suddenly.

" And she is dead ? "

" Five years ago," Batjushka answered, " Yes, Maria Alexandrovna."

The stranger as he fell behind, crushed a cherry unconsciously between his fingers so that they were stained red with the juice, and his heart began suddenly to throb uneasily so that it hurt him.

" To-morrow you also will go, Paul Karlovitch," Batjushka said. " You came to survey the land and now already you must go. What do we know of you ? Nothing. Not even whether you are married or no ? "

But before the stranger had time to reply, Batjushka had rushed away to drive off a bevy of ducks with his juniper stick, and the stranger had reached the house before the old man, breathing heavily, overtook him.

In the dining-room the table was richly bedecked. Pies and smoked flounder were followed by baked sour milk and roast duck, cherries and tea rounding off the meal. In the intervals, madeira was served from a dust-covered bottle. Batjushka ate slowly and in silence, Matushka hardly touching anything, only sitting at the end of the table, gay with the animation of a true Russian, excited almost to tears, chattering incessantly.

The air was thick with dust and hospitality.

The stranger ate with a fine discrimination and

carefully, like a person bent on losing no particle of enjoyment, but although to all appearance he was fully taken up by this pleasing occupation, the uneasy movement of his hands betrayed an inner nervousness.

" Was your daughter Maria Alexandrovna ever in St. Petersburg ? " he asked suddenly with perfect calm.

" Almost a year," Batjushka answered, with a tinge of surprise in his voice. " She took singing lessons there. Why do you ask ? "

" For no particular reason. . . . I was once acquainted with a Maria Alexandrovna in St. Petersburg. . . . But I seem to remember that her parents lived in Livland."

" We removed here only two years ago," Batjushka said. " They transferred me, an old man, most unfair. . . ."

" Perhaps it was just our Masha you met there," Matushka remarked. " Was she beautiful ? "

" Very," the stranger answered.

" Masha was beautiful," said Matushka. " Everybody admitted it. She was like me."

" Jevgenia Ivanovna was a beauty in her youth," Batjushka said smiling, as though in apology.

" Was Maria Alexandrovna married ? " the stranger asked.

192

" She died eight months after her marriage,"
came in a trembling tone from Matushka.

" There were no children then ? "

" She died in premature childbed, that is,
she . . ."

A warning preventive glance shot from Batjushka's eyes, but Matushka went on :

" There was no need for her to die. . . . But
there are dreadful things, things of which one
cannot speak."

" Yes, thou art right, silence is better," echoed
Batjushka.

" Pavel Karlovitch will soon be hundreds of
versts away." Matushka broke out excitedly.
" You see, her husband, Pichelbaum the merchant,
used her badly and therefore she died."

" Let us leave the subject," came in Batjushka's
cracked bass.

But bright spots of red now flamed in
Matushka's cheeks.

" Masha had had a lover before her marriage,
during her betrothal, though we knew nothing of
it and even now have no idea who. . . . How
could we know here, beyond the sea, what she did
in St. Petersburg ? For years I have borne hate
in my heart without knowing whom I hate. . . .
If my daughter had been drowned I would say

nothing, I would understand and submit, instead of rebelling. . . . I would call it Fate, a high green wall of water. But now I hate some one unknown to me. I could forgive the wave that drowned her, but not the human being who destroyed her."

" One must forgive people also," Batjushka said.

" I have already forgiven Pichelbaum. . . . He had been wronged, that I can understand. . . . The one I cannot forgive is the other, the unknown. . . ."

" One must, one must " . . . Batjushka said, nodding his white head.

" No, no," Matushka responded with heat. " A human being has eyes I can soften, ears I can plead to, a hand which I can grasp in prayer, I can attempt to move him by my tears. . . . But Fate, that is a wet, green wall of water. . . ."

" Calm thyself, beloved," Batjushka soothed her, himself in tears.

But Matushka continued :

" When I think that perhaps I have seen him, that with these hands—these hands—I have set food before him, that his fingers have touched the latch of my door . . ."

" Did she never disclose his name ? " came

the subdued voice of the guest. The cherries
lay untouched on his plate.

"Never—never. She was not like me, she
took after her father in that and could keep silent.
I said to her a little before her death, 'You might
speak now, Masha, and ease the load upon your
soul, and for us also it would be easier.' She
only looked at me and shook her head. And so
she died."

All were silent. It was almost twilight in the
room. No one touched the food, which grew
cold on the generous table.

Suddenly, through the silence and gathering
darkness, the stranger spoke :

"Has Pichelbaum married again ?"

"He has been married again for many years,"
Batjushka replied.

Matushka's eyes, tearless and as though dried
up, were fixed in contemplation of that one
thought.

"I must reveal everything to you, once I have
begun. . . . You ask only a little, and still I
feel I must tell you all, against my will. You see,
we knew nothing of it all, I swear to you, we
thought we were giving Masha away as pure as
from my side. . . . But Masha had had a lover,
a lover—and for that Pichelbaum beat her. He

beat Masha when he was drunk, and sometimes, even when sober. Pichelbaum told us himself afterwards, he accused us, who knew nothing. He would not even believe the child was his own, hating it even before it was born."

"By your leave, Jevgenia Ivanovna," the stranger interrupted her, "may not this man of whom you speak have been Fate itself for her? Perhaps it was written in the stars at his birth that he was to crush the happiness of your family, even against his wish?"

"Even then, even then," Matushka responded excitedly, "it is natural to wish for revenge on the person involved; one wishes to punish him, to humble him, an eye for an eye, a tooth for a tooth."

"And why should the duty of revenge fall on you, Jevgenia Ivanovna?"

"No revenge, no revenge," hummed Batjushka.

"But I am a mother. I would know him in a thousand by my mother's instinct, my hate would betray him to me."

"Are you so sure of that, Jevgenia Ivanovna?"

Matushka's black eyes rested in confusion on the stranger's nervous fingers.

"You do not believe it, Pavel Karlovitch?"

"I have not said that I do not believe it. Have you ever suspected any one, then?"

" Never."

Silence followed. The eyes of all three swept slowly from face to face in the dusk, which hid their features.

Like the needle of a talking machine, bringing dumb discs to life, slowly revolves in grooves as fine as hair, the sharp needle of memory began to move in their souls, cruelly, inexorably awakening old melodies to life.

" It is dark. We must light the candles," Matushka said in a toneless voice.

She groped for the matches. It seemed ages before the familiar scrape of a match was heard. She lighted two candles in silver candlesticks that stood on the table, her hands trembling as she did so.

Suddenly, her glance fell upon the stranger's pallid face and with an uncertain voice, as though feeling her way in the dark, she asked :

" What was it you said a while ago, Pavel Karlovitch—did you say you also had been in St. Petersburg ? "

And in the short space between question and answer there came upon them full knowledge of the bond that was to bind them together for all that was left of their lives.

Bernhard Riives

A YOUNG OFFICER WHO FOL-
lowed the punitive expedition to the Baltic
Provinces told this story :

" We had arrived with sixty bluejackets at one
of the parishes on the Estonian coast. The parish
we had just quitted had been one of the worst
hotbeds of the revolt, almost all the baronial
manors were in ashes ; we had therefore shown
the utmost rigour. To tell the truth we were
tired of blood, both the bluejackets and our
commander, not to speak of myself. One never
gets quite used to it, in course of time one sickens
at the sight of it, except when one is drunk with
blood.

" Without any preliminary agreement or even
a word among us we had decided to let mercy
go before justice this time. With all the greater
reason as in the whole parish only one manor had
been burned down, and this, as was proved, was
the work of a band of rebels from elsewhere.
Smaller offences against the law had of course
occurred in numbers. The tavern had been
compelled to close down, new rates of pay for truck-
servants had been enforced by threats of a strike,
and the signatures of the terrified landowners

obtained for these contracts, revolutionary meetings had been held and speeches made. We arrested and cross-examined a dozen or so of the men, but the chief culprits, the agitators and promoters of the meetings had all disappeared. The farmer who had led the deputation of the truck-servants was our only more important capture. In spite of many warnings he had remained on his farm, from which he was brought by the blue-jackets to our military court. His name was Bernhard Riives.

" We discussed the situation with a couple of the barons and the vicar of the parish, and all of these exhorted us to leniency, to which we ourselves were inclined. Only the baron, who had been visited by the truck-servants, stood out for the death sentence for Bernhard Riives, as a warning to the parish. He seemed to nourish an old grudge against the man, who, as we were later to hear, had dared to set up again the ancient boundaries of his farm, which crossed one of the baron's meadows. After a short exchange of opinions he agreed, however, to alter his demand to two hundred strokes with rods, the limit of our sentences in this parish.

" We, therefore, had the farmer Bernhard Riives called in. He was a tall peasant, with calm

square features fringed by a full beard.   The alert
and intelligent look in his blue-grey eyes was at
once self-assertive and crushed.   He showed no
sign of fear, though he seemed to expect no good
of us.   He was in no way insolent, still less
fawning; on the contrary, he seemed to have
grown beyond these qualities that long slavery
brings forth.   In all his being there was a sugges-
tion of efficiency of an unconscious power to rule
over others, his heavy shoulders seemed created
to push others ahead.   He was one of those peasants whose children often form the first generation of a new cultured class.

" Our decision, as I have said, was already made,
but for form's sake we proceeded to examine him.

" Had he incited the truck-servants to go on
strike ?—Yes.   Why had he done so ?—Because
their conditions were intolerable.   Had he directed the truck-servants' meeting and written out
the new agreements ?—Yes.   Had he followed
them to the manor ?—Yes.   Why had he taken
on himself the leadership in this matter ?—
Because, having himself been at school for a couple
of years, he held it to be his duty to help others
who had not had his advantages.   Had he said
at the manor : ' If you do not sign now, you will
do so within a week in a different kind of ink ? '

—No, he had used no threats whatsoever. Had he been at the Parish Hall tearing down the Holy Image ?—No, that he had not done.

" All his answers were given with certainty and in a level tone, but at the same time with a kind of indifference, without hope, as though he had guessed the formality of the examination. His wise, grey eyes never rested on any of us.

" A few witnesses were next called. Without exception all spoke well of Bernhard Riives. He had purchased his farm free himself, and paid the greater part of the debt, a thing unusual in the Western part of Estonia. He had been employed in many positions of trust in the parish and had always shown moderation and sense. The only evidence against him was that he avoided both the church and Holy Communion. On the whole, he seemed to be without enemies.

" It devolved on me to read out his sentence. He was brought in again and stood before me in his sheepskin coat, open at the front. For the first time I felt his glance rest on me and although my own eyes were directed to the paper in my hand, I could feel the whole time the gaze of those searching and intelligent eyes. I remember myself wondering whether he understood Russian.

" I read, therefore, the sentence first in Rus-

sian, and as I am fairly well acquainted with
Eſtonian—I am from Narva—translated it immediately into that language.

"When I reached the words 'two hundred
ſtrokes with rods' I heard him grit his teeth. I
glanced up at him and saw that he was pale and
looked wild, as though his usual self-control had
deserted him for a moment. But he said not a
word.

"I gave the order for him to be taken away.
As he went out of the door, I saw his shoulders
shake as though with the ague.

"The smaller offenders were punished firſt.
I ſtayed away from the place of punishment ; my
nerves seemed in a ſtate of collapse and I hoped
devoutly that all would soon be over.

"I had ſtayed behind alone in the room, where
I sat arranging the documents in order. Suddenly the door opened and Bernhard Riives thruſt
his way in, held tightly by two sailors. His
appearance alarmed me and againſt my will my
hand went out to my loaded revolver.

"He was terrible to see. His cap was missing,
his clothes torn in many places, as though he had
juſt been through some hand-to-hand ſtruggle,
the blood poured from a bayonet wound in one
cheek. All the self-control resulting from the

high level of peasant civilization he had achieved was gone, he seemed to have ſtepped backward many generations towards the warlike inſtinĉts of his race.   His dignity and his air of superiority were, on the other hand, as before, and in like manner his unconscious leaderlike qualities ; ſtanding there he looked like a chieftain from heathen times.   But the fierce madness that had peered out of his eyes while his sentence was being read out had gone, and in its place was an immovable, frozen ſtare.

" ' What do you want ? ' I asked him.

" ' I will not allow myself to be flogged,' he answered with calm defiance.

" ' Your sentence has been proclaimed,' I said.

" ' Even then—it is not a sentence fit for me— I am not a slave to be beaten with rods ! '

" ' You were nearly sentenced to death, man,' I said.

" He ſtarted, was silent and looked at me.

" ' You can thank the commander for his mercy, that you got off with two hundred ſtrokes,' I continued.   ' You may go.'

" I commanded the sailors to seize him, but he shook himself free.

" ' What now ? ' I shouted impatiently.

" ' I will not be beaten,' he repeated.

" ' Man, weigh your words,' I snapped at him. ' We can have you shot.'

" ' If that is all—shoot me,' he said.

" I went to speak with the commander. A man's life is worth but a kopeck, I thought, and a queer emptiness, a sense of being cut loose from life, scattered my thoughts, making them seem disconnected and unreal. . . . By an effort I tried to control them, to force them to follow their ordered, military course, the only possible one for them. And still a momentary sense of weakness possessed me. . . . What were we to do ? We were both helpless. I dared to suggest that we should let the man off altogether, but in my inmost mind I too understood that by such a step our authority would be shaken in the eyes of the peasants. It was impossible, there was no way of avoiding the punishment.

" The commander took the matter easier.

" ' Let him choose himself between a flogging and death,' he said. ' That will soften him, you will see.'

" I went again to Bernhard Riives and reported the commander's decision to him. He listened in silence.

" With all the means in my power I tried to reason with him.

" ' Have you a wife ? ' I asked.

" ' Yes,' he answered simply, as in the examination.

" ' Any children ? '

" ' Yes—five,' he answered.

" ' Then in God's name—think of them, man.'

" I was afraid for him and at the same time I desired keenly to break down his obstinacy, the inmost reasons for which were not entirely clear to me. And yet something in him caused me to salute him in secret.

" He did not answer, but seemed to be battling with himself.

" Listen to me, now,' I said, ' gather your wits. You see I am working for your best. You are a strong man and can well endure the punishment, you will be laid up for a week and then all will be well.'

" ' I am not afraid of that,' he said.

" ' What then, why don't you answer ? '

" ' I cannot. That is all, my nature won't let me, I cannot. I can die, but I cannot allow myself to be beaten.'

" ' You have always been beaten,' I said. ' When you were slaves, you were always beaten. Your father was flogged, and your grandfather before him.'

" 'That is true, we have always been beaten,' he agreed. 'But I will not be beaten. I was born free.'

" He had found himself again. The old equanimity, sprung from his peasant civilization, that I had noticed at the first sight of him, appeared again in his lofty, square features.

" 'Your children, man. Five children who will be left orphans if you are shot.'

" 'Better for them to grow up fatherless than the children of a slave. Shoot me.'

" His wish was fulfilled. I was not there when he was shot. I did not even wish to see his body, which was taken away by his wife and the oldest of his sons, neither did I wish to hear anything of his last moments.

" But my opinion is this : in this peasant, this Bernhard Riives, seven centuries of slavery straightened its back."

The Death of Org

I

OVER THE NEW COW-HOUSE ON
the manor a roof of shingles was being
built. It filled a whole side of the yard ; the
wall of rough grey stone rose stoutly as the wall
of a church, the unglazed windows gaped long
and narrow. Only half of the roof-tree was in
sight—it was a noble log of pine that from time
immemorial had heard the wind sough through
its branches in the manor park. But now a man
sat astride of it and hammered in nails among the
shingles.

Such a cow-house was unheard of in ten provinces. Even the drawings had been brought
from afar across the seas, from the land where
the cattle also had come, and a builder speaking
strange tongues had measured out the foundations in the company of the lord of the manor.
The very stones for the walls were not from anywhere near by—grey stone they were, hard as
iron. Three hundred head of cattle were to
find room in the new cow-house, as the owner
intended to increase his cattle next year again.
There were new-fangled objects, the purpose of

which it was not easy for the uninitiated to guess ; a heating-apparatus that propelled hot air along pipes the whole length of the building ; a system of ventilation that kept the air sweet by means of cross-currents, and special pipes that poured out an unending supply of fresh water.

All the other buildings on the manor estate were put in the shade by the new cow-house, even the main building itself, which, despite its size, was low and old-fashioned ; not even the parish church could compete with the new cow-house in grandeur, as this cattle-church had also its tower, many feet high, holding the reservoir to which the water was to be pumped. And one morning a cross actually appeared on the spire of the new tower, only to disappear in some mysterious manner before the arrival of the bailiff. But after this occurrence the new cow-house was christened the " church."

The cows, the glossy-coated, peaceful givers of milk, passed their future home each morning— lowing at the great windows and butting their horns inquisitively at the corners of stone.

It was a very hot day before midsummer. The men up on the roof sweated as they hammered fast the shingles, high up on a level with the crowns of the hundred-year-old oaks and limes. The lord of the manor had just finished his morning round of inspection and departed ; the work progressed more slowly, the men slackening as the breakfast-hour approached.

On a pile of shavings against the wall of the cow-house stood Org, the former cow-herd of the manor, his feet stuck in shoes of birch-bark. During the last two years he had given up the herding, receiving a small pension from the manor as an acknowledgment of his lifelong toil in its service.

But in spite of his pension, Org still followed the cows in summer for his own pleasure. A constant attraction drew him to the bog-rimmed slopes, where he sat on a tree-stump, working upon the grey bark of the stunted birch that grows in the bogs and watching the younger men run in their turn to drive away the cows from the bog's edge.

He swore fluently at the cows, scolding them like beings with the power to understand his words at the first hearing ; angrily the guttural oaths gurgled in his throat, but fierce and rough as were his words, he never struck a cow.

From the time the building of the new cow-house was begun he was never seen elsewhere. Already at the digging of the foundations he had been present, his shoes of birch-bark flapping slowly and regularly about the chosen site, where he had taken the edge of a sun-dried log as his perch. He spoke seldom with the workmen and bore their jests calmly with never a quiver of his jaw that sprouted grey stubble. To himself he may have muttered now and then, but he asked few questions, only sat throughout the days with a short pipe between his teeth. At times he would even enter the building and gaze with suspicion at the tower and the many taps, the meaning of which was beyond his comprehension. A well-meaning man would sometimes start to explain to him their purpose, and then he would grunt with pleasure, filled with respectful admiration. At times the wags would joke with him, stuffing him with the most unbelievable lies ; the old man at first believed them, but in the end came to know that he was being fooled, and the would-be wits had the whole stock of his oaths poured over them.

For the day-milking, however, which was carried out at the other end of the yard, he would climb down from his pile of shavings, and when the maids were too far off to hear, he would speak to the cows, addressing each one separately, calling them by his grandest swear-words, as though dealing out a pet name for each of them. Then in a series of grunts he would tell them of the new cow-house, and how they were to live like barons, so that even the priest had to be satisfied with a more humble palace, except on Sundays, when he stood in his pulpit.

They would be able to have an uninterrupted view through the large windows and gaze on the highway for their pleasure—just as noble ladies sitting behind the drawing-room windows in their gay clothes peep at the passers-by. He chattered to them also about all the new fittings, the water-pipes and the ventilators—while the immovable eyes of the cows fixed him with their goggling stare, and their jaws chewed unceasingly; farther away the steady trickle of milk was heard.

It happened once that some one told him of another baron's stables, where the stalls were of precious black stone; it spoiled his temper for a couple of days—no animal, if he had his way, should be better housed than his cows.

According to his custom he stood now again on his pile of shavings, on which the sun shone so fiercely that one might have expected it to burst into flames; on the roof the hammers clanked regularly, and the roof-tree grew shorter as the white shingles crept forward and hid it.

A man came driving a load of stones up the hill. The horse baulked midway in the rise, and stopped suddenly. The man struck with his whip at the thin flanks of the horse, under the skin of which the muscles could be seen braced for a new effort.

" Come up there, who asked you to be a horse ? —should have been a cow if you wanted an easy time of it."

The man's quip carried to the roof of the cow-house, whence came in answer a burst of laughter from many throats : " Should have been a cow, poor old horse."

Org on his pile of shavings twisted his mouth also into a smile, to him it was a happy jest.

But suddenly a man burst out on the roof, knocking a nail into the shingles as he spoke :

" Better for many people to have been born cows, if food and drink in plenty are what they want. Cattle have churches built for them, but the truck-servants . . ."

It was a wandering labourer, a town-dweller who had spoken.

A single attempt at laughter was heard that died in the laugher's throat.

For a long time no one spoke.

But on the roof it was as though something

had taken root and had begun to grow, as poisonous fungi spring up swiftly in mi&t and rain.
Over the men's heads a sombre cloud seemed to
take shape, despite the flaming sky ; they worked
suddenly as though under a thunder-cloud threatening deluge at every moment. In each of them
it ripened separately, grew rapidly like a flaunting,
poisonous toad&tool, no one broaching his thought
to another. But to every one it became miracu-
lously clear on the in&tant : here I sit on the ridge
of the cow-house and hammer a high roof for
cattle, and live myself with my children in a pig-
&ty. And they did not know which to wonder
at mo&t : the thought itself or the fa& that they
had only ju&t now become aware of it.

The trifling je&t of the horse and the cow fell
like a spark into the dry grass. But it seemed
relu&tant to bur&t into open flame, smouldering
in&tead as though deep in damp moss.

The hammers clinked—clink—clank . . .

Ju&t as on uncountable other workdays—no
change whatever. Only a my&terious brooding
beat down on the roof, a heat that seemed to have
come from the sun into the hearts of the men and
there burned, withering them and blinding them.

Org on his pile of shavings wondered at the
silence that had fallen on the roof, and he with-

drew after a time into the shade afforded by the corner, where he lay in a half-sleep, his shapeless cap drawn over his eyes.

The sun poured down its fiery rays, while everything sprouted and waxed under them. Something huge and amorphous ripened in its heat, something primordial, a deep unrest stirring the deeps below the surface of faces outwardly unmoved, the first attempt of men to grasp their own nature and their relations to the rest of things.

A couple of days later a deputation of the truck-servants waited on the gracious lord of the manor with a petition : "that they might be housed as well as the manor cattle."

II

Old Org dreamed a remarkable dream one December night. He stood on the unfinished walls of the cow-house, and suddenly the workmen began to paint them over with red ochre. Also the roof received a blood-red coating, so that it glowed fiercely. Org went into the cow-house and there he received the greatest surprise of all—the men were there also, brush in hand, and with paint-pots beside them, and what were they doing but daubing the cows red, confound them !

They were juſt at work on big Kirjo, the cow with a white ſtar on her forehead. The cows were being painted bright red, so that their backs and flanks gleamed like flames of fire.

Org was juſt about to say, " Stop that, you rascals ! " but juſt then one of the men made a threatening move at him with a brush that dripped red.

At that he awoke. The room was lit up by a ruddy glow. He rose and opened the door, before him ſtretched an open field, only a little snow lay as yet on the ground. Behind the foreſt of fir the sky blazed red.

Org's thoughts moved slowly. Suddenly he felt as though a spark had dropped from some-where ſtraight into his brain.

The manor was on fire. . . .

The spark bit deep, and burned into his brain, swift and ſtinging.

Never in his life had he been compelled to think so quickly. Then suddenly it became clear to him —the cows !

A low growl rumbled deep in his throat as he tied his shoes of birch-bark to his feet with des-perate haſte.

Now he was already on the way towards the red light, which drew him as a flame draws a moth. He had never looked upon himself as being in any way a person needed in the world, but now he felt suddenly that he could not be done without. The manor might well be attended to by others, but who would save the cows? . . .

He cursed without ceasing as he ran; the cap fell from his head and rolled before the wind along one of the plots; he ran on. . . .

He was in the rearmoſt yard of the manor and was near to ſtaggering from the speed with which he had run. The cow-house was ſtill ſtanding in its place, its high roof cutting darkly across the blaze of light that came from behind it.

The manor main building was on fire.

Org gave thanks to God that it was the main building and not the cow-house. He felt at the same time that he had hurried too much; he was panting and choking for breath.

The lowing in the cow-house grew louder, a swelling chorus of terror and pain.

Org felt the burning spark in his brain again. But he went firſt to the main building to see whether help was needed. He saw at once that it was beyond saving : the building burned from all its four corners.

People crowded the yard and the garden.

" There is water in the garden lake," he said

to the first man he met. But the man only looked at him with a madman's vacant stare, smiling a peculiar smile, and did not answer.

From the wing, where the fire was less fierce, furniture was being carried out into the yard. Org dragged himself there to see whether he could be of assistance. Already a huge pile of furniture had been gathered in the yard—gilded sofas and chairs with silken upholstery, carpets, portraits of knights and high-born maidens with bared throats.

Suddenly, Org with amazement saw that some one was setting fire to the pile with a lighted torch.

At this, the spark in Org's brain burst into open flame. He who had never thought much began all at once to think, as though a sudden light had burst upon his mind.

Suddenly he understood that all these people had not collected, as he had first believed, to put out the flames, but to light them.

With their own hands they were burning down the manor, which their ancestors at one time with their own hands had built.

And they were burning not only the manor but something else, something fearful that was as a weight over them, something very, very old. . . .

It seemed to them as though this shapeless heavy and terrible something flew upwards and melted away in the air like smoke, as though it had already ceased to exist. . . .

They looked at the smoke and were as if they saw it disappearing with the smoke. . . .

Org felt ready to weep at it all : at them and at their misery.

But again he awoke to the purpose that had driven him there.

" Why do the cows bellow so ? " he asked.

" They are unmilked these last two days," answered some one who rolled a large tun of wine.

Org understood this also ; to-day he understood everything. These people who were casting off the weight of seven centuries from their backs— these had no time to remember that two hundred cows were unmilked.

He began to run hurriedly towards the cow-house. No one hindered him, every one was engrossed in his own occupation.

He went in through the side-door.

An ear-splitting bellowing filled the building, an incessant lowing, one unbroken vain appeal for help.

Some of the stronger cows had torn themselves free from their stalls, and were ragging round the stables, goring each other until the blood ran.

But the majority lay as though in fever, eyes burning, panting, lowing without ceasing.

All were joining in the uproar : some softly whinnying, plaintively, as though aware of the hopelessness of their condition ; others frantically, with strong-muscled necks outstretched. . . .

The hay in the mangers had been finished, some were gnawing in their hunger at the wooden walls of their troughs.

The low-toned, even whinnying nearly drove Org mad. Those which submitted to their fate had eyes staring with fever, great eyes as immovable as glass.

He drew near to one : it turned its head as in pain, its eyes flickered wearily ; suddenly it was overtaken as though by a fit of madness, and drove its long horns with a crash into its wooden manger.

Org tried its udders ; they were hard as stone, hot and swollen.

He began to milk the cow, straight on to the ground, on the straw.

But at the same time the hopelessness of his task became apparent to him ; he could not alone milk two hundred cows. . . .

His head felt as though on fire, and the feeble

whinnying seemed to thrust itself into his brain, echoing in his ears and ringing through his head.

The whole cow-house seemed to have become transformed into the nethermost hell, where everlasting lamentation prevails.

Org felt that his wits would leave him were he to remain in the cow-house.

He began to run backwards and forwards along the platform that stretched the length of the cow-house, cursing horribly.

Had the cows ever done anyone wrong ? was it their fault that they lived in a stone-built church ?

It seemed to him as though the plaint of all these animals battling against fever and hunger was aimed at him—as though all the lowing, bellowing mouths reached out towards him. . . .

A cow fell down on its side right before his eyes in cruel agony, as though attacked by cramp, froth falling from its jaws. . . .

Org could hold out no longer ; he fled—as though the whole horde of cattle had suddenly turned upon him and were following him in fury, their horns lowered to gore him.

Outside it was as light as day. The old spruce firs in the park were burning at their crowns like tall pillars in an illumination.

Org stopped every one he met.

"The cows—the cows," he kept on repeating.

His tongue would no longer form any other word, it covered all his despair.

But he met only delirious, fanatical eyes that stared at him without understanding, eyes blinded by fire, themselves burning with strange wild fires.

"The cows," he stammered.

He could not have said whether the men he met were drunk, and if so, whether with vodka or with something else.

Something stronger than the intoxication of mere spirits seemed to possess them.

All that he understood was that no one even intended to help him.

But suddenly he saw a figure climb up along the corner of the cow-house on to the roof, a lighted splinter in its teeth.

His brain seemed to burn up, so swiftly did it move to grasp what was happening ; only an unfettered, blind fury remained behind. . . .

They were going to burn the cow-house. . . .

If he had seen his own cottage being set alight it would have hurt him less. . . . Even the church might have been burned to ashes before his face. . . .

Now all ran towards the cow-house in gathering numbers, their shadows waxing long upon the snow.

A curious emptiness had taken possession of Org's head, as though all that had been in it had oozed away.

He ran back into the cow-house, no longer knowing what he did ; he bellowed, lowed, as if to drown the bellowing of the cows, surrounded by chaos. . . .

He began to loose them from their halters, and one after the other they gathered in a mass, rushing with the fury of despair at one another, dealing fearful wounds, crushing the weaker under foot. . . .

But not one had the sense to charge towards the open side-door.

Org roared at the top of his voice, loosening chains and couplings.

From the roof the crackling of the shingles was heard, it had taken fire.

The animals, half demented with fever, were as though gathered into one many-headed, many-horned monster.

A biting, suffocating smoke began to drive in clouds into the building.

Every thought of himself had left Org's mind,

hardly could he have said who he was—he was as part of this gathering of cattle.

He shouted commands to it and ordered it about; he was its leader, but now he seemed to be speaking its own language, a language it understood.

One last logical thought blazed up in his dimming brain:

" Why don't they save the cattle—such expensive cattle—why don't they open the main door and drive out the animals ? "

And then in answer came his last coherent thought:

" From the cows it all began : they lived better than the truck-servants, and this is their revenge on the cattle."

The fire glowed already through the roof, burning embers began to fall.

The frenzy of the brutes rose to its highest pitch. . . .

But Org was no longer disturbed by the hellish din. He took part in it himself ; he ran round the cow-house, reckless of horn-thrust or kick.

Suddenly he stumbled over something and fell. . . .

He staggered up. Before him lay a dead cow, newly calved.

The calf, quite moiſt yet, ſtaggered on its feeble legs and reached out after its dam's udders.

Something awoke at that in Org, no longer a thought, but a kind of inſtinct ; he took the calf in his arms and began to carry it towards the window. . . .

Everything else became suddenly of no meaning to him, his ears ceased to hear, and for him silence reigned around.

Only the wet body of the calf he bore in his arms was real to him.

He bore it as one bears a child.

The heat in the cow-house was suffocating.

He reached the window, which was not at any height from the floor. He tried to open it, but failed to find the catch, and broke the window into fragments with a blow.

He lifted the calf towards the window, its soft nose brushing his hand lightly—now it was level with the window. . . .

Then something heavy and flaming fell upon him.

He dropped on the cement floor of the cow-house over the bleating calf.

The White Ship

IT HAPPENED THAT SPRING, THAT close on two hundred peasants of Järvamaa, of the sect of Maltsvets, having given notice, quitted their lands at the manor, left their seed unsown and the fields untilled and set out to wander towards the Tallinn coast, to await the white ship whose coming their prophet Maltsvet had certified. And to those who tried to frighten them with the manor-lord's anger they made speech as one man, that a heavy and deep sleep would befall all who attempted to prevent the chosen of God from departing for the new Canaan, where milk and honey overflowed.

When they bivouacked for the last time in the meadows of a certain village, the people came in great numbers to stare at them, as everywhere where they had shown themselves, but they bore the witticisms of the crowd unflinchingly, making no answer, following the example of our Lord, and obeying the command of their prophets, both in the loosened hair of their women and in the abstinence of their men. As only a few hours separated them from the spot where they were to await the marvel and the glory of the Lord, they prayed and chanted long into the night, strength-ening themselves with the manna of the Word and delving in the Holy Book, in which their pilgrimage had been foretold of old. Their horses rested at some distance, near the wagons.

When the Maltsvets departed the next morning, Maie, the young wife of Merits, the village merchant, stood before her baking-oven, her bare arms coated with dough, her hair moist and curly at the temples with the heat. Hearing the noise and the rattle of wheels, she hurried to the door, afraid for her two little sons who only a moment ago had played in the yard, and sought without finding them among the crowd. Then suddenly she was aware of a voice, clear and not to be misunderstood : " See, two stand in the fields and grind, and one is taken," and her heart was filled with a great unrest on account of these words, like unto dough to which yeast is added, so that she forgot her two sons, and likewise the bread in the oven, and went indoors, staggering as though overcome by sleep.

Long she stood before the open oven, forgetting to close its doors, her arms hanging loosely at her sides, the scent of ripening bread in her nostrils. The house was empty, all having run out into the village road.

Thus she stood, until the silence awoke her.

226

She ran to the shop window and saw the road lying empty, the dust, shot with sun-gold, settling slowly on the ground.

She turned into the room again and, still as one asleep, began hurriedly to gather together a few things—anything within reach—but suddenly ceased and left everything on the table. Not even a shawl did she tie round her head. Her hands were sticky with dough and her dress thick with flour as she ran swiftly into the road. She remembered her two sons, who had played near the well, remembered the bread in the oven and the unlocked shop door and ran on, sure of finding the pilgrims in the road-way.

As soon as she had overtaken them, all doubt fell from her and she felt a desire to speak, as on the evening before she had heard a couple of women speak in the Maltsvet camp, forgetting her timidity and saying in a great voice :

" Verily, the prophet Maltsvet will send a vessel to the Lasnamägi shore for his believers, and he commandeth his people to gather in a meadow, where the young grass groweth, and the ship will be white like a summer cloud, white as the sea-foam."

But many around her made inquiry : " Who is this ? " And others answered : " She is not

of the Maltsvets, as her dress is of many colours
and her hair is plaited."

She made answer to them all :

" Why do ye ask ? I am no one ; I have neither
name nor children, neither husband nor home."

At that they were satisfied and asked no more,
understanding that God had spoken through the
mouth of this woman, to strengthen His chosen.
Then as the sun was beating down on her unsheltered eyes, a woman was moved to offer her a
shawl, but she refused it, casting loose instead her
hair and letting it flow freely after the fashion of
the wives and daughters of the Maltsvets ; and
her hair was so long and curly that it hid her
coloured petticoat.

Space was made for her on a wagon, but she
said that she preferred to walk, offering her place
to a child the soles of whose feet were blistered,
while she herself supported the weary and carried
the babes of exhausted mothers in turns, herself
only a while ago feeble and delicate. Food was
proffered her, but she shook her head, and to all
questions made reply that she hungered and
thirsted but for righteousness and the heavenly
vessel, thrusting back the hands which held forth
bread, so that all who heard her words wondered
at her belief. And for the rest of the journey she

spoke no more, answering only the most necessary questions, so that she was suffered to remain alone; but her eyes were still opened wide and full of distant visions that only she could see, keeping silence regarding them.

Some said : " See, the Holy Virgin of Tiskre is among us."

Others, who had heard the Virgin of Tiskre speak the year before, answered : " Not so, this woman is younger and her hair is like unto honey before it becomes set."

But there were also some who said : " Is not this Maie Merits, of the general store ? Was it not her husband who sold me a barrel of herrings last St. Bartholomew's Day ? Had she not two tiny children at home ? How comes it then that she is amongst us ? "

Others again chided these, saying : " Has not the prophet Maltsvet also another name, like the names of us others ? Has not he also shared in all manner of worldly tasks, such as the keeping of a tavern and the milling of flour ? Has he not bartered horses and been as one of us ? Why should we then draw back from this woman, even if she has at one time done otherwise than declare the miracle of the Lord. Away with such talk."

The more worldly among the believers asked :

" Has she even a written permit ? How can she intend to depart with us to a distant country ? Has she the letter signed by her husband and the lord of the manor and confirmed by the Governor ? "

There being many other such vagrants among them, however, without written permits, no one made to disturb her, all being exalted with high hopes and their tolerance great.

Arrived at the Lasnamägi shore, near the town of Tallinn, they all seated themselves in a growing meadow thick with yellow flowers, in happy expectation, being altogether nearly three hundred persons of both sexes, including children and suckling-babes. And excepting a week's provision and the most necessary cooking utensils and clothes, they had nothing with them. The horses used by them on the journey were sent back, having been sold already before their departure ; their houses and other property, their grain and their cattle having also been exchanged for money.

Hardly had they halted before a tall and blind woman began the hymn : " At last my eyes behold you, Holy Land," conceiving that they were already at the goal. Her lips were parted, her nostrils trembled, breathing in the perfume that was not, the scent of flowers which never had grown in the beds around her yard, and she stretched forth her hands as though to warm them in the rays of a warmer sun, her eyes, covered with grey cataract, blinking helpless as she strove feebly to see the vineyard preached by the prophet. Yet when her mistake was explained to her, she sorrowed not but let herself be led to the water's edge, where she stayed patiently waiting, holding the hand of her guide, so that she might not be lost in the multitude when the signal for departure was given.

Then, because Maltsvet their prophet had forbidden them to kneel, they prayed standing upright, with faces turned to the blue sea whence help was to arrive, all clothed in garments that were black and grey, rarely white, likewise according to the direction of the prophet, and the hair of their wives and daughters hanging loosely as it grew.

Later, they sat down again on the rocks lining the shore, one of the readers opening the Bible, in which the whole of their journey was prophesied and written down particularly for them, they doing nothing unbidden by the Book nor refraining from anything commanded by the Book.

And it was written : The peasants of Järvamaa were oppressed in divers manners, both in body and soul, and sorely tormented by their alien masters, as were the children of Israel by the Pharaohs in Egypt.

And it was written : God would awaken a prophet for His people groaning in slavery and beneath the whip, whose speech would be sweeter than honey, sweeter than that of the Moravian readers, and the name of this prophet was John II or Maltsvet, also called by his earthly name of Juhan Leinberg.

Further, it was written : Maltsvet would lead his children out of slavery in Egypt to abodes more blessed, arriving among them in a white ship.

Obeying the commands of their spiritual leader, they had cast aside their garments of many colours and all delight to the eyes and plaited hair, the young maidens their head ribbons, and their lips were pure of wine and strong drink, of the flesh of swine and of the smell of tobacco.

But where their Canaan was situated, none knew. They had heard their prophet, in the course of his wanderings through the villages, speak of a far, warm country, set aside by God for His chosen, where there was neither master nor slave, no frosts at night and no snow, only green vineyards, in eternal sunshine and fruit-giving rains. They had also heard the name of this country, but it had passed away from their brains. All they knew was that the prophet Maltsvet had departed thither before them, and according to his promise would return in a white ship to the Lasnamägi shore to fetch them.

For this reason they would not permit the children that evening to gather twigs, and no woman set a kettle to simmer on a fire between two stones, neither did anyone open his bundle or sack as on other evenings, nor did anyone prepare a bed for himself, for his wife or for his children, these being looked upon as signs of faint belief, a tempting the forbearance of God. The bigger children lay side by side on the sand, like lambs in the fields ; the smaller cried themselves to sleep in the laps of their mothers.

The blind woman sat immovable, her sightless eyes closed, her fingers round the wrist of her guide, feeling the beating of the pulse therein and awaiting the quicker leap of the blood, which was at once to give sign to her of the approach of the vessel on the horizon.

But the woman who had escaped from her husband and children and whom no one knew, had washed her arms white in the sea and sat now among the others, her hair hiding her face from her companions, and she remembered no jot of what she had been or what she was, being as one born again that day.

The mothers with many children took pains to be sure that their children would be near them when the ship came and that none were lacking, gathering their young around their skirts as a hen gathers her chickens.

Then Maie, directing her glance straight into the sun, felt a sudden blindness, and all around her faded in a mist of light, and from this milky vapour, which filled the whole horizon, the pale contours of a white ship began to show.

She saw it quite clearly, not with inward glance, but with bodily earthly eyes, floating slowly across the waters, that grew calm before it, with no splash of oar, leaving a long silvery wake that was loath to disappear—its sails swelling, frail as white clouds in the sky.

" I see it—I see it," she shouted in a ringing voice.

The crowd surrounded her ; she was seized by the shoulders, and her hair fell thick and golden over her face.

" I see the white ship," she said.

"Where is it? Show it to us," she heard shouted around her.

At that she felt the longing of all those hundreds flow into her until her soul seemed overfull. She seemed herself to disappear, as though the boundaries of her soul and body had given way ; her spirit dissolved to nothing, and she was loſt with it, but suddenly life awoke within her for all who ſtood around, drooping and in pain, with a great and bitter yearning. Their hope and their tears collected in her as in a reservoir, and she saw and waited for all.

"Can ye not see, ye blind ?" she said. "Open your eyes, the white ship promised by the prophet approaches us."

And at the same time her limbs turned ſtiff, and the women received her body falling to the earth, and placed it on the sand, where she lay fainting, bedded on her long hair.

But the men took up their packs and carried them to the water's edge, and women cried to their offspring, babes wailed, and many young men waded as far as they might out into the shallow water, while yet others raised their voices in a hymn of welcome, but the ſtronger refrained from pushing the weak aside, and whoever was accompanied by an aged and infirm father or mother, supported them, all being joined together by mutual love.

When thus they had waited for two hours, many were weary, and they said to one another : " It was but an omen. The strange woman whom no one knows has prophesied. She has been granted a sign before us."

And others again said : " To-morrow or the day after the ship will come."

The women cared for Maie, sprinkling water on her face until her senses returned to her, but she said no further word the whole evening.

Before dawn many of the children bemoaned the cold, and mothers bared their bosoms, warming them with the heat of their own breasts and, doffing a part of their garments, covered with them those that still shivered. When day began to dawn, a strange weakness befell them and many slept, but for the most part they kept awake, fighting against exhaustion, the new day rekindling their belief and expectation.

They prepared a meal for the children, refusing to eat themselves, refreshing themselves with cold water from a spring, and feeling no hunger.

At midday idle and curious crowds from the direction of the town began to gather at the meadow's edge, asking questions and talking

236

with the pilgrims. As always, they suffered all mockery in silence, and making no answer, exercised themselves in patience and forgiveness, sure of the speedy discomfiture of their mockers.

The following day their hopes were calm and certain, and not one doubted, and all murmuring was far from them. In the evening their actual waiting began, and so certain were they of the speedy arrival of the vessel that each gathered hurriedly the articles scattered about during the day, so that time might not be wasted when the call came. And they extinguished every fire but one, left burning as a signal for those approaching from the sea.

Many times their belief was strengthened by the growing of their numbers, for new brethren in belief and awaiters of the white ship arrived from the coastal parishes, and room was made willingly for the new-comers, and what was left to share was shared. But from the fifth day onwards they began to cook regular meals, imploring, to be sure, forgiveness from the Lord for this mark of unbelief and impatience, knowing too that not only the children were begging for food, but that many grown-up people were faint with hunger. They, though at first ashamed and battling against the pangs, gave way in the end,

237

gnawing first in secret at a crust of bread, and then proclaiming in a loud voice to all and sundry that surely it was not the will of God to starve them to death.

When the first week was over, close on five hundred souls had collected in the Lasnamägi meadow and on the shore. The weaker beginning to bewail their weakness, they took turns at night to watch, so that there never lacked those who gazed seaward day and night, that the oil in their lamps might not be exhausted as befell the foolish virgins.

Maie wandered among them, and in her brain dwelt a dim remembrance of something she could not recall. Her thoughts stopped always at the moment when she felt the crowd around her, but what was beyond that moment it was impossible for her to say. At times thoughts not her own came to her, like fragments of some lost and distant being. Sitting on the shore, and watching the children roast their half-naked limbs in the sun, she felt a desire to go to them and stroke their heads, and when she half-unknowingly fondled the children's hair, the feel of it awakened in her a sense of familiar things, which she had surely lived through before, but where and when ?

Unable to decipher these thoughts, she drew

away from the children, only to return to them
again, feeling in their company nearer to her lost
self. She divided among them almost the whole
of her food, for her own frame seemed to need
scarce anything, and to feel no fatigue, although
she never slept beyond midnight, and faith radi-
ated from her.

Each evening, at sunset, a feeling of unrest
came over her and her heart throbbed, and when
the others gathered expectant round her, her
limbs stiffened, as in death, but from her lips a
flood of words poured, while her spirit wandered
in far lands.

Then those listening to her saw her as though
she waded through tall wheat, and her hands
weighed the ears thereof, and they saw her shake
out the grains into her palm and praise their
whiteness, and later they saw her climb upwards,
and now she plucked grapes from vines for them,
the juice streaming between her fingers, until she
herself and all around her were intoxicated with
the golden stream, and her rapture moved them
also.

And she asked them :

" Do ye thirst for earthly or for heavenly blessings ? "

But as the memory of their long days of labour

and of all manner of slavery awoke in them, and as heavenly blessings had been held out to them for hundreds of years, they answered now :

" We thirst for heavenly blessings, but look, we long also for those on the face of the earth."

She then answered them :

" Both shall be given to you."

She spoke to them of the prophet Maltsvet, whom she had never seen, and she described him to them as though she saw him before her with earthly eyes and plainer than any among them, so that they asked in wonder : " Where had she seen the prophet Maltsvet ? Can this woman see what is hidden to others ? "

And their waiting became a rapture and their belief grew stronger.

But one evening the sky became overcast, and a thin rain descended throughout the night. They covered the children for the night and no one murmured, all being hardened and well used to all manner of weather. Then as the rain fell throughout the next day and the next and likewise the fourth, they fetched straw and hay from a neighbouring village, while those of the coastal parishes read the signs of the wind and assured the others that the rain would soon cease, so that their only sorrow was they could not keep the signal fire burning night and day, in spite of all their efforts.

But the rain continued for six days and six nights, and the low-lying meadow, unable to absorb any more water, changed into a quivering quagmire. Then hardly had the rain ceased when the wind veered into the north, and on the open shore where they were gathered fell a storm from the north, which swept their camp for three days. The first to murmur were the mothers, on account of their shivering children, saying : " Let us at least erect shelters for these little ones."

To this the men whose belief burned strongest answered : " Perish the thought. Are we unable to bear these slight hardships for the blessedness promised us ? Shall we build huts to sleep in, while the ship of God draws ever nearer ? "

They closed their ears and hardened their hearts, but the mothers of children were obstinate and did not cease to beg, and the fathers of children were more easily moved than the others, and thus at the end of the second week a few shelters had been erected on the sand and covers drawn over them.

The air was again fine and warm, it being the month of June.

One of the Maltsvet children had discovered the nest of a water-bird between the hummocks on the shore, and visited it each day, saying to itself : " When there are five eggs in the nest, the white ship will come."

But when there was no longer room for another egg in the nest, he said :

" When the young birds break out of their shells, the white ship will come."

When the nest was full of young seafowl, he said :

" As soon as they have learned to swim, the white ship will come."

And each day he visited the nest, forgetting to spy out seawards as a matter no longer of any account.

At the beginning of the third week the two-year-old son of a fisherman from Kolgarand fell ill with fever and convulsions and died in the lap of his mother, who wailed and stormed alternately. Her husband nailed short unplaned boards together, and bore the coffin on his shoulder to the town, but the mother followed behind, and the white ship in which her little son was leaving her gave her no joy.

And returning from the town she was still more dissatisfied, beginning to complain in a loud voice and say she needed no white ship, but wanted her son back again, whose sickness was a result of the cold and wet nights. But her husband, who was pious and Godfearing, hurriedly silenced her before she could heap sin upon sin, and after that she dared no longer to speak her thoughts aloud, her lips moving instead in a silent babble of words that none understood.

From that time onwards, the mothers began to fear for their children, of whom there were many in the camp, and some proposed that the children be sent away, but others refused to consent, wishing all to set forth together to the promised land.

The yellow flowers lining the meadow, where these had not been crushed underfoot, gave place to violet, followed by red, and finally blue, and when one morning the child went to the seafowl's nest, it was empty, and for the first time for weeks he looked out seaward, but the open water stretched wide and sunny, and all he could see was a covey of downy young seafowl, but no white ship.

Sure as he had been earlier in his belief, the greater was now his disappointment as he, weeping, inquired of all he met : " Will the white ship never come ? "

And each one to whom he turned comforted him, begging him wait with patience, but the words had been spoken and a child had been the first to say them, and the words had not fallen on empty air, as many words fall.

The white ship still delayed, but in its stead came all manner of diseases from the earth and the water, likewise from the air. Gout appeared, twisting their limbs into strange shapes, boils and malignant growths, and severe griping pains accompanied by a wasting fever attacked many. Those who had quenched their thirst with the rusty water of the ditches lay raving on the straw in the clutches of fever, their heads white-hot, their brains filled with mirages, striving to break away from their watchers in order to go and meet the white ship conjured up by their delirious eyes. Those nursing them followed the gaze of the feverstricken, holding them back but full of envy for those who were at least happy in their visions.

The milk of many women nursing their off-spring dried up, and now the turn came for suckling-babes to fall sick, to be followed by those a little older. In many families all the children and even the adults lay ill, nine or ten children dying at this time in the laps of their mothers who were lost in prayers or doubt. But there were also those whose belief only grew the stronger at each obstacle.

One day, when Maie had strayed to the highway not knowing whither she went, she saw a man approaching along the road with heavy and dragging footsteps, and all against her will she awaited the comer, but her face was still without life as of one who walks in her sleep.

When the man came abreast with Maie, he was greatly astonished and turned pale, but Maie looked at him as at a stranger and did not greet him.

At that the man said softly : " Maie, dost thou not know me ? "

And Maie answered : " Truly, I do not know thee, but see thee for the first time to-day."

The man said : " Thou art become thin and sick. Come, I will take thee home."

But Maie answered : " Thou art mistaken, I have no home, no husband, and no children, and my speech is of those who are the Lord's."

She turned to go, the lustre fled from her golden hair, which was as though faded by rain and sun.

The following day she saw the man again, on the other side of the highway, where he sat as though waiting, calm and dusty. And in the evening, just as she felt the spirit of God come down over her and she had already beckoned those standing near, she suddenly became aware of the man once more, standing this time among the Maltsvets. Then all at once her limbs, already half-stiffened, relaxed, and she stood staring at him, a thought knocking incessantly for entrance at her brain. And she said to them all :

"To-day I cannot speak," and went down to the shore, and gathered seashells in the sand, and when she returned the man had gone.

The weather was fine and warm, and in the field there was no shade, the sun burning them in the unsheltered meadow, and they suffered from the sun as previously they had suffered from the cold. The heat made them sleepy, so that their only desire was to sleep, watchfulness becoming a burden.

But already in the third week their provisions were finished, no one having conceived the time of waiting would be so long, and all believing the white ship would be laden with food. Their sons fished along the shore, and at first were beaten by their parents, but at last none hindered them, nor could they prevent their children from straying to the highway, where bountiful and curious persons gave them alms.

At first they purchased bread and fish from passing peasants, those better situated sharing with the poorer as long as there was anything to share, all being members of the same chosen people. But they were many and their money melted away rapidly, and the day of hunger drew nigh.

Then one and another in the camp began to murmur and say : " Has Maltsvet forgotten those who believe in him ? Does he sit alone near the fleshpots of Canaan and refresh himself with the fullness of the vineyards, what time his followers are tortured by hunger and all manner of sickness ? "

Others said :

" Has the white ship been shipwrecked before it reached the Lasnamägi shore ? Has some misfortune happened ? "

And there were also those who said : " Why deceive yourselves and others with empty promises ? Go home and plough your empty fields. There is no white ship, and Maltsvet is a scoundrel and liar."

Others rebuked in horror those who spoke so, saying :

"Our belief is weak beyond words, and the Lord trieth us."

247

But when hunger had weakened their bodies scorched by the sun, their mood changed. They sat in turn in dumb despair, letting the dry white sand trickle through their weary fingers, and at this time it was the same to them whether it were morning or eve. The fishers from the coast began to think of their nets, which they had given away at their hurried departure or sold for trifling sums, and when in the evenings they saw the men from the adjoining villages go forth to fish, they followed with their eyes the little sails as though seeing in them the promised white ship, and they longed for the work which they had left. The ploughmen gazed at the black empty fields, where not one green blade of rye reminded any of the labour of the spring, and it was as though the barren land lifted up its voice in accusation against the men who had left it at the mercy of the weeds. They then suffered more from their craving for toil than from hunger, and their eyes were full of fear and implored pardon of the passers-by of whom they begged news of the state of the harvest and the size of the catch.

Maie's speech was tangled and strange at this time so that not nearly all could follow her thought, although her trances lasted longer and she could speak without ceasing for two long hours. They

knew then that she sought as one asleep for
something lost, often pleading, often wailing
aloud, with eyes closed, that she now could see the
ship but very dimly.

And again there were many among them who
said : " What do ye await ?   Let us return home
before we perish."

But when the thought came to them, that their
old life would begin anew, as though nothing had
happened in the meantime, they were stricken
with horror to the depths of their souls, awakening
from their torpor, and knowing that they had sold
everything they possessed, that there was neither
wall nor roof they might call their own, and that
no morsel of land would now be theirs.   Then
it was that they were unable to grasp that God
had forgotten them and forsaken them, after they
had given up their all, and a feverish hope flickered
anew in their brains worn with hunger, and there
was no longer any limit to their expectation.

And now the throng of spectators that collected
round the camp grew from day to day, large
crowds wandering out from the town, some to
mock or to pity the pilgrims, but the greater part
merely curious.   Enterprising cheapjacks did not
fail to erect their booths at the meadow's edge,
and as once it was with the Temple of Jerusalem,

so the sky-roofed temple of the Maltsvets was the scene of marketing and bargaining throughout the day, and the air was filled with noise and jest and merriment, until midnight put a stop to the revelry.

One night the blind woman sat sleepless with her hand stretched out as though to seek the warmth of the oven wall, and her ears seeking hungrily in the grasshopper's tweet for an echo of the chirping of the house-cricket, for the sounds she was wont to hear at nights in her home. Then awakening her guide she said : " What is the white ship to me, whose eyes may never behold it, and Canaan where my footsteps will be as uncertain as here ? Is it not one to me whether these darkened eyes be warmed by the glow of a hearth-fire or by the sun of a warmer land ? " After which she lay down to sleep, but in the morning she suffered herself to be led round the camp, saying her adieus to each, bemoaning the leanness of their hands, and no one attempted to stay her when she turned towards the highway.

The same evening, many of the younger men complained aloud of the poorness of the broth and held council together, and in the dawn they had disappeared, some one having seen them set off towards the town. The others waited for them until evening, but when the sun set and none returned, each understood that it was vain to wait for them longer.

Then the wife of the fisher from Kolgarand, who had kept silence ever since the death of her child, arose and went through the camp, saying to all who wished to hear, but especially to the mothers of small children :

" Why do ye vainly try God's patience ? Is it because ye wish Him to destroy you with all your children ? Can ye not see that He has turned His Face from us ? "

In the evening she departed and many with her, but her husband, who was a pious man and firm in his belief, stayed behind, and the number of those who stayed with him was still large, and in truth they were in doubt what to do, death from starvation threatening them in the Lasnamägi meadow, the whip and slavery awaiting them at home.

So once more they probed their souls, blaming their unbelief and their transgressions for the trials sent them by the Lord. For what signified the sending of a white ship to the Lasnamägi shore for the Lord of Lords ? He needed only to say to a white fine-weather cloud : " I send thee down as a ship to the Tallinn coast, where

My chosen people who have found favour in My sight await thee." Or what signified it for the Lord to command the greatest man-of-war in distant waters : " Turn in thy course, for thou art needed on the Lasnamägi shore."

Perhaps they had drawn down God's wrath by over-indulgence and the lust of their eyes ? Was it indeed possible that He still demanded some sacrifice of them ? They were ready to give up anything, did they but possess it. For five weeks they had borne hunger and sickness in the Lasnamägi meadow, but their spirit was still willing should the Lord demand more.

They prayed as they had not prayed for weeks, with the intensity of despair : " Demand of us. Give us a sign that we may know Thy will." Memory of the times that followed the call came back to them, of the time when Maltsvet wandered from village to village, waking souls, expounding a new belief, and when the desire of their hearts had been to cast from them all that before they had lusted for.

And then they who had starved ever since weaned by their mothers collected the last remains of their provisions and burned them, to appease God Whom they had offended. They poured the milk and small beer on the sand, whoever still possessed such, breaking their cooking utensils that none might be tempted to use them. A great exaltation possessed them, and they stopped up the springs, choking them with gravel, hardening their hearts to the cries of starving children and showing no mercy to the sick.

They saw again the white ship, as in the first days of their waiting, and as the Spirit had prophesied through the mouth of a woman, and they knew that were their belief but firm enough a miracle would happen. They saw it approach on the horizon, between the squat men-of-war and merchantmen of the harbour roads, a ship of silver, white as a seashell, ready to receive them all and, riding lightly on the waves, carry them to the abode of the blessed.

If ever the yearning of Man finds favour before the face of the Lord, in truth the sacrifice of these people was great.

But on the evening of the third day of their fast, when all were assembled on the shore, it came to pass that a man from Järvamaa began to hold his head and cry out like a drunken man, though not a drop of vodka had passed his lips, and in the sight of all he began to run along the shore, in the direction of the fishing-boats. They saw him stumble and run anew, waving the whole

253

time with his arms, though the sound of the waves prevented them hearing his words. When he reached the boats, they saw him push off a boat and row out to sea, with a single oar.

All were silent with wonder, standing still and waiting for what should happen.

" He rows out to meet the white ship," some said.

But suddenly they saw him throw away the oar, stretch out his hands as though to something they could not see, and step over the gunwale of the boat as though walking on dry land, and he disappeared from their sight.

Then a great cry ascended from their throats, a cry long and despairing, and for a long time they ran along the shore, not knowing of what they did. And only some few had power to think and to row out and begin to grapple for the body, which at last, when the next morning had come, they found and placed on the shore on a bed of last year's rushes.

At that the scales fell from their eyes, and all became aware that their pilgrimage was ended, and they began to gather together their possessions before departing, seeking Maie that they might empty the vials of their disappointment on her.

But Maie sat on the bank of a ditch with her

back turned to the others, her hands drooping and weary in her lap, in which she had gathered flowers of blue and red.

The lustre of her golden hair had vanished, but her eyes were still motionless, like those of one who walks in her sleep.

Though no one spoke to her, she knew, sitting with bare feet in the meadow ditch, that all waited for her to open her mouth and speak.

But there was no longer anything to say to them.

She tried to remember who she was and whence she had come, breathing the perfume of the hand-orchids in her lap, and fingering helplessly their roots which were waxy-white as the hands of a dead child ; but she remembered nothing.

A child of the Maltsvets who had been on the highway among the idlers from the town came to her carrying a large slice of newly baked bread that was still warm.

And as Maie had always been gentle with the children the child broke off half the bread for her.

Maie grasped it as one asleep, when from the newly baked soft rye-bread a familiar scent rose to her nostrils, awakening at first a fierce hunger, but the next moment she saw before her an open baking-oven and loaves baking within.

Her hands flew to her head, a thought flashing

through her brain : " For the Lord's sake the oven must be closed."

In a moment the voice of some one she could not see said in her ear : " What art thou doing here ? For what dost thou wait ? "

And at that her strength failed her, her body drooping, and memory returned.

She saw her two sons playing near the well in the yard, the coat of the eldest torn at the elbow. The door of the shop was open and from an open barrel came the odour of rotting herrings.

She remembered her husband, her sons, her everyday tasks, the chamber behind the shop and the bread baking in the oven, and her hands went instinctively to her unplaited hair, while her heart turned sick with longing.

" There is no white ship," she said, rising to her feet, weak and staggering as after some great illness.

And no one lifted a hand to prevent her going, each having his own griefs, wherefore Maie Merits was able to pass through the crowd to the highway and to begin her journey home, having waited for five weeks for a miracle in the Lasnamägi meadow.